Dirt

David Vann's first book of fiction, the international bestseller *Legend of a Suicide*, has now been translated into eighteen languages and has won ten prizes, including best foreign novel in France and Spain. His novel *Caribou Island* is an international bestseller. He is also the author of two bestselling non-fiction books, and has written for *Atlantic Monthly*, *Esquire*, *Sunday Times*, *Guardian*, *Observer*, *Sunday Telegraph*, *Financial Times* and other magazines and newspapers. A former Guggenheim fellow, National Endowment for the Arts fellow, and Wallace Stegner fellow, he is currently a professor at the University of Warwick. For more information visit his website at: www.DavidVann.com.

ALSO BY DAVID VANN

FICTION

Caribou Island
Legend of a Suicide

NON-FICTION

Last Day on Earth: A Portrait of the NIU School Shooter
A Mile Down: The True Story of a Disastrous Career at Sea

'People often say of thrilling books that they read them in a single sitting; with this extraordinarily alarming and convincing piece of work, I had no choice . . . Possibly his biggest achievement is never to allow you to guess quite how far it – or he – will go. No author is better at making you lose your literary balance and a large part of his brilliance is that he knows how to adjust the level of derangement to just short of most disturbing . . . It's Galen himself – a superbly uneasy and memorable creation – who rocks this novel from start to finish. Intelligent, imaginative, unruly, possibly unhinged and borderline repellent . . . Vann's gift – his quest, almost – is a willingness to explore the unimaginable, the unthinkable, on the page. He is the real thing – a mature, risk-taking and fantastically adept fiction writer who dares go to the darkest places, explore their most appalling corners. I haven't read a novel as rough and shocking or, importantly, as wise and warm as this one in a long time.'

Julie Myerson, *Observer*

'The characters in *Dirt* read as archetypes, figures in a Beckett play: Galen, the boy who seeks escape; nursing-home-grandma, whose fading memory suggests the unbelievability of the past; Galen's mother, Suzie-Q, who wants what all mothers want: to be loved, not bothered; aunt insane, who demands the money she knows is locked in a trust; Galen's teen cousin, a sadist who uses the one thing she's got to tease virgin Galen, thus representing the temptations of a fallen world. The resulting sex scenes are stunning, a dirty taboo pitched to comic perfection . . . The last pages of *Dirt* are lit by a berserk energy. It's as if Vann has pulled off the trick of putting us inside a Hitchcock maniac . . . When you finally put this book down, break the spell and walk away, you're left with a deeper resonance, a lingering sadness.'

Rich Cohen, *Financial Times*

'The last hundred pages of Dirt are as audacious and uncompromising a piece of writing as I've read in a long time. Vann is a brave writer, daring to write about and depict things that most other authors would baulk at, but that's what makes him so good – that unflinching eye for the darkness you could potentially find in any of us, given the wrong chain of events. If you want to feel good about the human condition, go elsewhere. If you want the naked, awful truth, then dive in.'

Doug Johnstone, *Independent on Sunday*

'A pitch-perfect, unflinching exploration of a family's brutal infighting... Vann's rendering of the everyday gratings of family life is pitch-perfect. But he's never shied away from the brutal and so the endless cycle of small family hurts is escalated into hatred and violence as Galen, his mother, aunt and cousin pit themselves against one another in an outlandish, horrifying and apocalyptic battle... A well-written, unflinching exploration of the often terrifying chasm between who we want to be, and who we actually are.'

Sunday Telegraph

'Broken families, and the violence and destruction that love can wreak, continue to be his abiding themes... So builds the dreadful climax and dark denouement of this brilliant narrative ... This is a novel of violence, destruction and ruin. There is no salvation. And yet Mr Vann's soaring writing carries it forward – a reminder of the beauty that can grace even the beastliest things.'

The Economist

'Past master of family dysfunction hits the spot – again... Vann really is a brilliant documentarian of folie de grandeur. From this point on, Dirt is unputdownable, thundering at breathtaking speed towards the shocking climactic act. Brilliantly chilling.'

Evening Standard

'Reminiscent of southern tales by Flannery O'Connor, John Kennedy Toole and Tennessee Williams. And while Galen's religious obsessions align Dirt more with O'Connor or Toole, it's Williams's world that the novel is otherwise closest to: the unforgiving, brain-invading heat; the incessant family squabbling; the autocratic patriarch (dead, but still looming in this case); the over-devoted mother; the furtive, incest-like relationship; and the failed, trapped central character, nevertheless convinced of his special gifts and destiny...Vann expertly establishes the frictive family's dynamics, and the first half's spiky pretension-puncturing dialogue is often as funny as Galen's disconcerting encounters with physical reality and the teenage temptress.'

Literary Review

'Vann is expert at writing about such family dynamics, the passive-aggressive behaviour, the explosive rows and outbursts, the festering grievances...Over the course of a few days, Vann expertly teases out a Greek tragedy's worth of issues, from lust and incest as the virgin Galen is powerless in the presence of his sexually experienced younger cousin, to the Oedipal relationship between Galen and his mother, to the damaging effects of Galen's efforts to distance himself from human emotion through his New Age beliefs and practices. What Vann does so well is to take recognisably ordinary characters and put them in critical situations...This is what gives his books their nightmarish quality – the feeling that these events could happen to anyone.'

Irish Independent

'Another dispatch from dysfunctional suburbia by one of the US's hottest writers...A morbid fascination with the family's eye-poppingly vicious interactions keeps you turning the pages...It's hard to forget.'

Metro

'His language is sharply funny, even as his characters enact a tragedy of Greek proportions.'

'Vann's sex scenes are unflinching, and what happens at the cabin ultimately delivers the novel and its characters into a traumatic culmination that leaves Galen irretrievably debased ...I won't give away more about the ending except to say you read it knowing: *I won't ever be able to forget this, even if I want to.* Vann has written a horror novel saturated with nuanced pain. Its dog pile of cruelties is insistently inventive. Its psychological acuity is ruthless. Its willingness to follow its characters into their self-made tragedies, the darkest extensions of their characters, is brave and brilliant...Dirt is showing us something unexpected, and unexpectedly stunning, as well.'

Dirt

David Vann

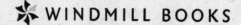
WINDMILL BOOKS

Published by Windmill Books 2013

2 4 6 8 10 9 7 5 3

Copyright © David Vann 2012

David Vann has asserted his right under the Copyright, Designs and
Patents Act, 1988, to be identified as the author of this work.

First published in Great Britain in 2012 by William Heinemann

Windmill Books
The Random House Group Limited
20 Vauxhall Bridge Road, London SW1V 2SA

Addresses for companies within The Random House Group Limited can be found at:
www.randomhouse.co.uk/offices.htm

The Random House Group Limited Reg. No. 954009

www.randomhouse.co.uk

A CIP catalogue record for this book
is available from the British Library

ISBN 9780099558743

Designed by Renato Stanisic

Printed and bound by Clays Ltd, St Ives PLC

DIRT

Galen waited under the fig tree for his mother. He read *Siddhartha* for the hundredth time, the young Buddha gazing into the river. He felt the enormous presence of the fig tree above him, listened for the no wind, for the stillness. Summer heat pressing down, flattening the earth. Sweat in a film covering most his body, a slick.

This old house, the trees ancient. The grass, grown long, making his legs itch. But he tried to concentrate. Hear the no wind. Focus on breath. Let the no self go by.

Galen, his mother called from inside, Galen.

He breathed more deeply, tried to let his mother go by.

Oh, there you are, she said. Ready for tea?

He didn't answer. Focused on his breath, hoped she would go away. But of course he was waiting here for her, waiting for tea.

Help me bring out the tray, she said, so he sighed and put down his book and got up, his legs cramped from being crossed.

There you are, she said as he stepped into the kitchen. Old wood bending beneath his bare feet. A roughness from varnish flaking off. He took the tray, the old silver, heavy, the ornate silver teapot, the white china cups, everything that depressed him, and while his hands were full she leaned in from behind and gave him a kiss, her lips on his neck and the little snuffling sound she did to be cute, which made him flinch and want to scream. But he didn't drop the tray. He carried it out to the cast-iron table under the shade of the fig, close against the wall of the farm shed with its small apartment above. He was considering moving out here, to get away from her, away from the main house.

His mother beside him now with the finger sandwiches, cucumber and watercress. They weren't in England. This wasn't England. They were in Carmichael, a suburb of Sacramento, California, in the Central Valley, a long, hot trough of crass, as far from England as one could be, but every afternoon they had high tea. They weren't even English. His grandmother from Iceland, grandfather from Germany. Nothing about their lives would ever make any sense.

Sit, his mother said. Enjoying your book?

She poured him a cup of tea. She wore white. A summery white blouse and long skirt, all white, with sandals. Thighs flaring, the bottom half of her growing faster than the top half.

Have a sandwich, she said. You need to eat.

The finger sandwiches with crusts cut off. Cucumber and cream cheese. Even if he had felt any appetite, this food would have been near the bottom of the list of all foods in the world.

You look emaciated, she said.

What he returned to was breath. Whenever she spoke, he returned to his breathing, the exhale, letting all attachment to the world slip away. He counted ten exhales, and then he sipped his tea, hot and minty and sweet.

Your cheeks are all sucked in, and it looks like you have bones in the front of your neck.

There are no bones in the front of my neck.

But it looks like there are. You need to eat. And you need to take a shower and shave. You're so handsome when you put in a little effort.

His breath coming faster now, anger always a flaring upward, a sense of broadening at his neck and shoulders, the top of his head gone. He could say anything in these moments, but he tried to say nothing.

It's just food, Galen. For chrissakes, there's nothing special about it. Watch me. And she raised a cucumber finger sandwich slowly in the air, a small square, and slowly pushed it into her mouth.

Galen looked down at his teacup, the tea a kind of stain in the water, darker toward the bottom. Wilted green leaves of mint, rough with tiny bumps. The world a great flood in which nothing would ever stop. It could not be controlled, it could not be held back. It was rising and compacting, pressurizing. School starts in a month, he said. I should be going to college. I shouldn't be spending another fucking year having high tea.

Well you're free to go.

We don't have any money. Remember?

Well, that's not my fault. We make do with what we have. And we live in this beautiful place, all to ourselves.

I'd rather live anywhere else.

His mother lifted her tiny spoon and swirled her tea, and Galen waited. Why do you want to hurt me? she asked.

The air was not breathable. So hot his throat a dried-out tunnel, his lungs thinned like paper and unable to expand, and he didn't know why he couldn't just leave. She had made him into a kind of husband, her own son. She'd kicked out her mother and sister and niece and made it just the two of them, and every day he felt he couldn't stand it even one more day but every day he stayed.

. . . .

AFTER TEA, GALEN WENT up to his room. The master bedroom, because his mother slept in her old bedroom from childhood. So he slept where his grandparents had, a long open room of dark wood, the floorboards oiled and worn. Wood up the walls forming a ledge at chest level. Old fabric above that, French with fleur-de-lis patterns in dark blue set in panels three feet wide, separated by dark beams that went all the way to the ceiling. And the ceiling a series of boxes in more dark wood, with a carved area above the chandelier. A place ornate and heavy, too grand for his insubstantial life, something from another time.

Galen's bed frame was made of walnut from this orchard. That was one thing that fit. He could go out and sit on the stump. But beyond that, he didn't know how anything had come to be or who he was supposed to become.

He walked downstairs to wait for his mother at the car. A circular drive in front of the house, attached to a long lane of hedge, overgrown now. Flowers in the middle of the circle, also overgrown. Thistle and high grasses gone brown in the sun. There had been a gardener, and there was still a weekly fund paid out for a gardener, but the fund was what Galen and his mother lived on. That and the fund for weekly maid service.

The car twelve years old now, a Buick Century 1973, with a long sweep back from the headlights. A boat. Painted metallic orange, a new paint job from a year ago, Galen's mother throwing away money. Let's do it, she'd said. Let's just do it.

The metallic paint a giant reflector, cooking Galen as he stood there without a hat or sunglasses, his skin gone dark and ragged. A few hundred feet away, a giant oak and cool shade, a wooden love seat, but Galen remained. Kept his eyes open as wide as possible in the glare.

Galen could feel the earth leaning closer to the sun, could feel the land shouldering its way forward, pulling the hot sack of melt behind it.

And then his mother emerged. Sun hat and several small bags in her hands, fumbling with the keys, carrying sixteen things though they were driving only three miles. Every day after tea they drove to see his grandmother in the rest home. Everything a production, and of every production his mother the star.

She smiled as she walked toward him, a wide, lovely smile, her best feature. A long walk from the door to the drive, a path bordered by lawn, some of it still green. The water bill for the sprinklers paid directly from the trust.

Here you are, she said. Shall we go?

For his mother, no bad moment had ever existed. They had not fought at tea. They had never fought. Nothing unpleasant had ever happened in her entire life. Galen never knew what to say. So he gazed at the hood, a blinding sun, and tried to stretch his eyes.

Galen, his mother said. Open your door and get in. Legs go first. It's not tough, and it really doesn't mean anything.

So Galen opened his door and put one leg in, then decided to put the other leg in without using his arms. He fell over with a hard *whump* onto the gravel, let his shoulder take the damage. His legs twisted over the doorframe.

For chrissakes, his mother said. I really don't have time for this today, Galen. She came around the car and lifted him up by his armpits, stuffed him into his seat, and closed the door, without slamming it.

You think you're cute, she said as she ducked into the driver seat. She closed her own door and they were off, crunching gravel down the hedge lane.

They have wonderful pumpkin pies at Bel-Air, he said as they passed the shopping center.

Stop, his mother said.

They really do have lovely pies, he said. It was what his grand-mother had said repetitively every day before his mother stuffed her in the rest home.

His mother was trying to ignore him, something she was not always good at. The pumpkin especially, he said.

His mother believed she was a good mother and a good daugh-ter and a good person, so she would hold back from saying any-thing ugly. She looked bruised, her face gone dark, the smile no longer there.

If only I weren't locked away in the rest home, he said. Then I might taste pumpkin pie again.

GALEN'S GRANDMOTHER WAS IN perfect health with the exception of her memory. Suzie-Q, she said when Galen's mother walked in. They had a hug, and then it was Galen's turn.

Galen didn't like to be hugged. His family was all women, and they were always hugging him, many times every day. He would have preferred never to be hugged again for the rest of his life.

Look at you, she said. My handsome grandson. Are you getting ready for school in the fall?

Galen's upper arms were pinned in her hands. He tried to let his arms relax, as if they were someone else's arms. But she wasn't letting go. Her face was very close. A different face now than a few months ago. New dentures, and somehow they had entirely changed her face, made rounder and softer and foreign. As if it had never been his grandmother but always someone else hiding in there.

Not this fall, he finally said. I'll be deferring a year.

She looked at him closely, examining his face and eyes, trying to remember, perhaps. What she couldn't remember was that this was now his fifth year of deferral. Yes, she said. Yes, of course, some time before you start. We talked about that. Always a good idea. Maybe travel a bit, see the world first.

The imagined year abroad in Europe, the well-off young man carrying a small suitcase and boarding ocean liners and trains, throwing open the shutters in a hundred old rooms to look out over spires and stone. Wearing a linen suit, drinking in cafés, chatting in half a dozen languages. What made Galen angry was the fact that it could have happened. If he'd had a father and a normal mother, parents with jobs, and a grandmother who hadn't lost her memory, the extra money from his grandmother could have made this happen. Instead it was paying for the rest home, metallic orange paint jobs, and a mother who would never work.

Mom, you're going to tear Galen's arms off.

Yes, well, his grandmother said, letting go. You know you're my favorite grandchild?

White hair curving down in a bob, blue eyes bright still. Favoritism wasn't very nice, really, but he did love his grandmother. He'd always liked her better than anyone else.

Thank you, Grandma, he said. You're my favorite grandma.

Mm, she said, and hugged him again.

The room was very small, shared by an older woman confined to bed. Her eyes were always wet, and she was smiling at Galen now, looking like she was crying.

Maybe we should go for a walk, Galen said. He had to leave this room. Linoleum floors and plain white walls, sliding plastic curtains around the beds. A place to die, but his grandmother was well. A shared room because his mother wanted to preserve as much of the trust as possible and it wasn't clear his grandmother remembered she had money.

That sounds nice, his mother said. We'll go for a walk in the garden.

Last one there is a rotten egg, his grandmother said.

So they made a little game of racing out to the garden. Waving to the nurses in the hallway as if they were going away for good. Galen's mother smiling because they were being special. Specialness was her favorite thing.

Ah, she breathed out when they hit the garden and stopped racing. She grabbed her mother's arm and leaned in close. That was fun, wasn't it?

The garden a cement courtyard with planter boxes on wheels. They could be moved all around, so it was never the same garden twice. None of the plants reached higher than five feet, and there was no shade.

Galen's grandmother gave him a big smile. He tried to return it, what felt like a lopsided little grin with his mouth closed, a bit of skin stretching. Maybe he had different cheek muscles. They wouldn't pull upward on their own.

Look at all the flowers, his mother said, and it was true there were flowers everywhere. They pulled up to a trough of petunias, white and pink and purple in the sun. Like little faces, his mother said.

What time is it? Galen's grandmother asked.

Oh, look over here, Mom, some lovely roses.

They walked over to the roses, red and loose and thorny. Galen leaned in close to smell. He liked the smell of red roses.

Like Ferdinand the Bull, his mother said.

Thanks, Galen said.

You remember Ferdinand the Bull, Mom?

But Galen's grandmother was looking around now, worried. What time is it? she repeated.

He's the bull who won't do anything except lie around and smell flowers.

Maybe we should go, Galen's grandmother said. It's getting late. We should go home.

Look over here, Galen's mother said. They have nasturtiums.

We should go home now.

Galen tried to focus on his exhales.

Which way is out? his grandmother asked, looking around. Sweat on her face from this heat, her shirt going dark. There was no shade. I can never remember which way is out.

This way, Mom. We'll go back to your room.

We need to go home.

Maybe we can play cards, Galen said, trying to be helpful. He couldn't bear any of this.

That's a wonderful idea, his mother said. Let's play a hand of cards, Mom.

I want to go home. Why won't you take me home?

When Galen and his mother returned home, Galen's aunt and cousin were waiting. His aunt standing at the door, his cousin Jennifer slouched in the wooden love seat under the oak tree. Like gangsters. Galen's mother pulled up behind their crap Oldsmobile.

His mother went to the door, and Galen walked over to his cousin. This oak tree with limbs stretching out fifty feet in every direction. They'd played here as kids, played endless hours with Barbies and G.I. Joes in the shade.

Hey, Jennifer said.

Galen tried not to look. But she had one foot up on the bench, knee bent high, and a short skirt, and he could see her panties, light blue, could see the smooth skin of her thigh. She was seventeen, and he'd been taking peeks like this for at least four years now, unbearable. He looked down at the ground, at the grass that was up to his shins.

Hey, she said. You're looking good. So hot. I love your "I'm never going to take a shower again" look. The homeless are so sexy.

You take enough showers for both of us.

True, she said. I like how soft my skin feels afterward. She ran her fingers along her inner thigh. It's unbelievable, she said. Do you want to feel?

Stop it, he said, and he walked away, into the house. The parlor, cool and dark, the shades drawn, and he stood in place a moment at the bottom of the stairs. The baby grand that no one knew how to play. The old photos on the walls. The wide dusty planks. He creaked up the steps to his room and locked the door. Pulled out a *Hustler* magazine and lay on his bed.

The pleasure the same as despair, a deep and awful need, and his imagination terrible. Samsara, the world of suffering. So he put the magazine down, stopped moving his hand, left his dick hard. He took his tape recorder off the nightstand, put the headphones on, listened to Kitaro. Closed his eyes to camels in the desert, long journeys across sand and wind and time. Felt his spirit reaching across lifetimes, across incarnations, felt freedom. This body only a dream.

The banging at his door, though, was not a dream, and finally he had to take off the headphones. I'm coming, he yelled. Jesus. The world's not going to end if we don't have dinner.

He pulled up his underwear and shorts, then decided to put on jeans instead. Jeans could hide a boner. Just being near her he'd have a boner instantly. There was no stopping it.

Coming down the stairs, what he felt was dread, the same as any animal being led to slaughter. Meal of a Hundred Humiliations, he mumbled to himself, because it was better to give it a name in advance. That could take away some of its power. He moved slowly, his bare feet on the wood which was almost cool compared to the air.

Why are you wearing jeans? his mother asked.

Felt like it, he said. All three of them looking at his pants.

In this heat?

He sat down. A long, narrow table for twelve. He was in the middle, across from his cousin, only a few feet away. His mother and aunt farther away at the ends. They were already eating, piggies in a blanket. And they'd put one on his plate, half a hot dog wrapped in dough, baked. Side dishes of ketchup and mustard.

You need to eat, his aunt said. Even your eyeballs are starting to stick out.

Galen closed his eyes. They were in an enormous hot valley, a dust bowl, the Central Valley of California, and what he hoped for was a twister, a hot, dry tornado that would build for three hundred miles and come through the walnut orchard to explode the house. His aunt and mother and cousin lifting in their chairs, winging through the air, shattered wood like shrapnel all around, the little piggies flung from their blankets.

Our heavenly father, his cousin said. Give us this day our cheeks and neck and other bits of flesh.

Stop that, Jennifer, Galen's mother said.

I think we should pray that poor Galen be made whole again.

I said stop it.

Suzie-Q, his aunt said.

Fine, his mother said. I won't reprimand your little angel, Helen.

Galen opened his eyes. Now that the crossfire had started, perhaps he was safe.

That's rich, his aunt said. Galen will be at your tit until he's fifty. Don't talk to me about coddling.

Galen smiled. He liked his aunt. She didn't hold back. He thought of himself clinging to his mother's tit, tiny baby gums but an otherwise grown body. He laughed, and then he liked laughing, so he stretched and developed it a bit, chortled and added little yelps.

Okay, Galen. That's enough, his mother said.

But Galen kept laughing, let it bubble forth, and somehow it fed itself and he was feeling much better, lighter and almost free.

His mother got up and left, and without her here to feed it, the laughter slowly wound down. He had tears in his eyes. Ah, he said. That felt good.

You're a freak, Jennifer said. But I kind of enjoyed that. You should consider the circus.

We're already in the circus.

His aunt smiled—or what was a smile for her, anyway, lips pulled straight back—and looked up toward the far corner of the ceiling, her arms folded. Well, she said. Well, well, well.

Galen looked down at the little piggy. He was vegetarian. He was also starving, deep cramps in creases that folded and stapled him from the inside. It hurt so much he had trouble sitting up straight. His mother knew he was vegetarian, and she had served him this. Red nub of hot dog poking out of dough. The side dishes condiments.

You do realize, his aunt said, that at some point you'll have to become something. You'll have to go to school or get a job or do something. You can't remain a child forever.

I don't know if that's true, Galen said. Look at my mom, for instance.

His aunt laughed. That's true, she said. That is true. Little Suzie-Q.

You're a trip, Galen said. I like you.

Well, his aunt said.

The pantry door opened and Galen's mother returned. Are we through now? she asked.

We've only just begun, Galen sang.

Jennifer smiled and put her foot up on his crotch under the table. Her bare foot on his jeans, held there lightly, feeling his boner grow.

How was Mom today? his aunt asked his mother.

She was fine.

Any details?

You should go yourself if you want details.

It's not enough that you're the favorite? And that you get to live in this house and collect the checks? You also have to be snotty?

You're not going to be invited to this house anymore if you behave like this.

No empty threats, please.

Jesus, Galen said. Listen to the two of you.

It's the only sound in the world, his aunt said. How could we hear anything else?

Jennifer pressed harder against his boner, pleasant at first and then it kind of hurt. He put a hand down to try to push her foot away, but she was too strong. He looked at her and she was smiling. Mascara put on too heavily, a child's makeup. Blue eyes bright as marbles. But what he always noticed most was the down, the actual down along her cheeks and neck. He could see the tiny blond hairs, so soft. Something he wanted to feel against his own cheek.

What are you two up to? Galen's mother asked.

Just a stare-down, Galen said. First one to blink has to stay here at the table and talk with the two of you.

Stop it, Galen's mother said. Jennifer, you look like a little tramp. And all of you have to stop it. Why can't you just be normal? Why can't we just be a family?

Galen sighed. Okay, he said. May I have the plate of piggies, please?

Thank you, his mother said. And she passed the plate. A dozen piggies in their blankets. Galen slid them all onto his plate and then he stuffed them in his mouth with both fists, hot doughy intestinal meat with the taste of butchery floors and tongues and hooves. His cousin laughing and his mother gone again and he kept stuffing and chewing and swallowing the little abominations until there were

only shards on his plate, the ruins of the feast, and then he bent
down to lick his plate clean, left the table with his stomach heaving
and lurched up the stairs to his room and bathroom to vomit into
the toilet. When he was done, he folded his arms on the toilet seat,
his mouth acidic, and he took a little nap. Closed his eyes and slept
on the toilet with the unclean water below, thought about dipping
his head in for a drink, and he would have done it if his mother had
been watching.

When Galen woke it was dark. The house silent. The time of peace. The way he wished the world could be. No people.

He had to shake his arm to get it to wake up. He flushed the toilet and brushed his teeth. Then he walked barefoot down the stairs, stepping as softly as possible, trying to walk with no weight. His body lifted in the air, gravity gone. This world a dream, the house made of memory. His mother as a child walking these same steps.

Out through the pantry, he walked beneath the enormous leaves of the fig tree, could smell its fruit, let his jeans and underwear and shirt slip to the ground, stood naked. The moon nearly full, and as he stepped around the farm shed into the walnut orchard, he saw the array of bones. Long rows of white trunks and branches all turned to bone in this light. Every branch hollow and too large, luminous. The leaves as shadows too insubstantial to cover.

Galen ran as he had read in the Carlos Castaneda books, let his bare feet find their way in the night, their own path, closed his eyes and held his arms out to the sides, palms up. The clods of dirt crumbling beneath his feet, rocks hard, small branches, leaves. All of it hurt and made him slow down, but he wanted to be lifted free. He wanted to drift over the ground without sound or feel, his feet held just above the surface by a kind of magnetism. Instead, his feet sank deep into furrows, stumbled and jolted, and he never knew what was coming next. He opened his eyes and slowed to a walk, put his arms down.

The moon the brightest of bones. Dark patches forming the open mouth of a snake, a small man sitting below, meditating. Always the same moon. It never revolved, never changed. Always this snake head and small man etched on a disc of bone.

The trees arrayed in obedience to the moon, lined up, reaching upward. Even the furrows responding to the pull. All of the earth extending, trying to close the gap. The air so thin, what was keeping the earth and moon apart?

Galen sat cross-legged, his lower back braced by a furrow, and stared up into the moon. His palms open on his knees. Long exhale, and breathe in deep. Exhale again. No thought, only this shining disc, this mirror.

But then he was thinking of his cousin, of the inside of her thigh, of her lips, of her foot pressed against his crotch. Samsara always there, always intruding. But perhaps it could be used. Perhaps it could provide some power.

Galen rose and put his hand on his boner. He stroked it a bit and then tried to run like that down the furrow, stroking with his right hand, his left hand held outward to the side, palm upward, a meditative pose, his eyes closed. He tried to let his legs guide him, tried to let the boner guide him, lift him above the furrows toward the moon. And his feet did feel lighter. He was gaining speed, the dirt falling away farther below, the air gaining a presence, and maybe that was the key. Not some sort of magnetism from the earth but a pulling from the air itself. The air was the medium, not the earth.

He tried to leave his body, tried to place his consciousness outside, to see himself from far away. White bone-legs running, like the tree trunks come alive.

But his breath was ragged, holding him to the world, pinning him here when he wanted to lift free. Tall weeds ripping at him, lashing him, a snag between his toes and he almost went down. He had to open his eyes and jog to the side to get around the worst patch. And this was the problem. Always an interruption. Whenever he was getting close to something.

So he stopped. Stopped running, stopped stroking. He tried to never come, because he'd read that a man lost his power when he came. But he really wanted to come. And he was tired of just his hand.

Galen lay down in the hollow between two furrows, curled on his side. Breathing heavily, wet with sweat, the air cool now on his skin. His forehead in the dirt. The world only an illusion. This orchard, the long rows of trees, only a psychic space to hold the illusion of self and memory. His grandfather giving him rides on the old green tractor, the putting sound of the engine. His grandfather's Panama hat, brown shirt, smell of wine on his breath, Riesling. The feel of the tractor tugging forward, the lurch as the front wheels crossed over a furrow. All of that a training to feel the margins of things, the slipping, none of it real. The only problem was how to slip now beyond the edges of the dream. The dirt really felt like dirt.

GALEN WOKE MANY TIMES in the night, shivering. The moon a traveler, crabbing sideways through the stars. Galen on the surface of the earth. The planet not to be believed, spinning at thousands of miles per hour. There should be some sound to that if it were true. Some thrumming or vibration. But the dirt was soundless, and it felt too light, as if the earth's crust were only a few feet deep. What Galen wanted was for the crust to crack so that he could fall through, fall thousands of miles flipping through empty space toward the center of gravity, accelerating, and then fall past the center toward the crust on the other side and feel himself slowing as gravity took hold. Until he'd reach the underside of the other side of the world and touch it lightly with his fingertips, then fall backward again. His feet would never touch ground, and that would be good.

Galen was so cold his teeth were chattering. But he didn't get up. He fell back into sleep over and over, and the night was an endless thing. Each night a lifetime, including the wait for the end.

And when the end came, finally, when the sky lightened, the black become blue, Galen was not yet ready. Too quickly the air would bake, the earth would bake, and the day would repeat itself. There'd be tea with his mother and the visit with his grandmother and the visit from his aunt and cousin. Galen didn't feel he could do it again.

He had to pee so badly he finally rose, sent an arc of piss toward a tree, then hooked his thumbs under his armpits and crowed a *cockadoodledoo* loud into the dawn. He strutted around naked, flapping his arms, warming up, calling in the day. His stomach an empty cavern, a pit shrinking him from the center. But he kept strutting, broke into a low run through the trees, then over to the main house. Stood beneath his mother's window, crowed as loudly as he could and stomped his feet in the grass.

Damn it, Galen, he finally heard. I'm up now, and you know I won't be able to fall back asleep.

Galen felt a smile, the real thing, happen across his face, his cheeks pulling themselves up. No stunted thing, his face not broken. He stopped crowing, walked over to grab his clothes from under the fig tree, and went in through the pantry. Quiet up the steps to his room, and he closed the door, took a shower to be clean finally, then buried himself under the covers, a warm nest, and fell deeply into sleep.

Galen woke with Jennifer's panties just a few inches from his face, thighs on either side of his head.

Good morning, cousin, she said. It's a sin, you know, to peek at your cousin. But you're always peeking. So I thought I'd give you a good, close look.

Blue silk, a different shade than the blue cotton yesterday. More tightly fitting. He could feel the heat. He tried to smell her, but she smelled only like soap.

He was afraid to say anything. He didn't want this to end.

The twenty-two-year-old virgin, she said. This is the closest you've ever been, isn't it?

Yeah, he said.

Why is that?

I don't know. Just not very popular, I guess.

And a mama's boy. You never leave this house.

People don't value the spiritual enough.

You mean freaks don't get laid. You can jack off. You can jack off while you look at me.

So he reached down and began pulling, squeezing tight, enjoying the ache of it.

I'm going to turn around, she said. So I can watch.

She stood up on the bed, which tilted like an ocean, and came back down facing the other way. She pulled away the blanket and sheet so he was exposed. He pulled harder. This view he'd never had before. The backs of her thighs and ass, so perfectly shaped, beautifully cupped, and the hollow and curve toward the front. The edges of her panties against soft creamy skin.

Can you pull your panties to the side? he asked. I wanna see.

No, she said. Not yet. You only get the panties for now.

Not yet, he said.

Why would you even want it? I thought you wanted the spiritual.

Galen's dick was harder than it had ever been. He stroked more slowly to prolong this, and he could see she was getting wet, the silk darker in the center.

You're getting wet, he said.

Yeah, she said. I like this. I like watching. I want you to come now.

So he sped up his hand and arched his hips, feeling every part of him drawn tight, and then he came and his neck pushed back and he shook with the pleasure. He opened his eyes again, her panties dark and wet above him, and he wanted her in his mouth. Please, he said. Let me see, or let me just lick.

Jennifer stood up on the bed, stepped down carefully onto the floor in her bare feet. No, she said. But that was fun. I like that. It's always nice to spend time with family.

Galen laughed. It felt good to laugh, and he tried to add the little yelps again.

You're a freak, she said. I'm leaving. But she was smiling, and Galen had never felt so good. When she was gone, he just lay there and smiled and stared up at the ceiling.

Then his mother was knocking at the door. Get up, she said.

We're having a quick lunch, and after that we're working on the walnuts.

Galen had forgotten about the walnuts.

September, he yelled. The harvest isn't until September. But she was already back downstairs.

It was only the end of July, but his mother would make them put out all the drying racks to inspect.

So Galen rose and cleaned up, then looked around for green clothing. He would dress as a green, unripe walnut. He had a green sweater and green rubber boots. What he was missing were green pants. But in the hallway closet, in the stacks that smelled of mothballs, he found two green towels. He doubled old belts around his thighs to cinch the towels into place, then pulled on the green boots.

Galen walked carefully down the stairs, and he felt like some old knight heading into battle. He'd carry a giant cucumber for a sword, or a spear of asparagus.

Mother, he said as he entered the dining room. I am Green Walnut, and I am reporting for duty.

Galen's aunt Helen shrieked with laughter, and Jennifer snorted her milk onto her plate. But Galen's mother continued cutting the crusts off her baloney sandwich. Fine, she said. Have some lunch, Green Walnut.

I hope my unripeness doth not offend, he said.

His mother quartered her sandwich diagonally and picked up one triangle. Today is a special day for me, she said. It was this time each year that Mom and Dad would put out the drying racks to inspect them. We'd start earlier, of course, at first daylight, when the air was still cool. And we'd work quietly. I'd feel the day heat up, and by lunchtime it was wonderful to stop and sit in the shade under the fig tree and have lemonade.

And don't forget the wine, Helen said. The wine started in those early hours, too.

We'd drink lemonade, Galen's mother said. And we'd have sandwiches, cut like this, and we'd be a family.

Until the bickering would start, Helen said. I'm not sure where you're fitting in the bickering.

Stop, Galen's mother said. Just stop. Why can't you remember the good moments?

Gosh, I don't know. Maybe because I wasn't the one prancing around being cute? Maybe because I was older and knew what was going on?

That's not fair.

Wake up, little Suzie-Q.

Galen poured himself a glass of lemonade and then considered the food options. Baloney and ham in plastic packets, American cheese also in plastic, saltine crackers in plastic, sliced bread in plastic. I think I'll have a plastic sandwich, Galen said.

Mom and Dad had their problems, but what you don't seem to understand is that we were lucky here, living in this place, working on the walnut harvest together.

Dad used to beat Mom. He'd beat her right in this dining room, and in the kitchen, and upstairs in their bedroom. What part of that are you not understanding?

He never beat her.

Oh, for chrissakes.

Galen didn't want bread and mustard, which was one option, so he decided to go for the crackers instead. He grabbed a handful of saltines and crumbled them into his half-full glass of lemonade. He used a fork to submerge the pieces of cracker and then he drank his lemonade while shoveling with the fork. Salty and sweet and not really all that bad.

His mother was still working on her sandwich, and there seemed to be plenty of time, so he fixed another glass. A bit heavier on the crackers this time, pulpier, more substantial. Fitting in a good meal before a day's work.

When his mother had finished, she rose to take her plate to the kitchen. She returned to the dining room and looked at them all, sitting there. For a moment, Galen felt bad. Felt guilty for dressing up like this and destroying her special day. She looked hurt, and he didn't like seeing that. Not really.

I'm going to start on the racks, she said. If any of you want to join me, you may. She had curled her hair. Long brown waves. And she was wearing makeup. Galen wondered if she had planned this for the special day, or if it had happened only because she was up early from his crowing.

And then she was gone. He realized he was standing. Green Walnut must make up for everything, he said. Green Walnut has been very bad.

Hallelujah, Brother, Jennifer said.

She deserves it, his aunt said. You're the perfect curse for her.

But Galen ignored them, sallied forth out the pantry door and walked stiffly to the farm shed, trying not to lose the towels, same path he had taken last night into the orchard.

He found the large bay door slid open. The green tractor, slim front tires, narrow ventilated snout. A thing of the past. But he tried not to be distracted. Stepped into the dark half of the shed, where his mother was hidden deep in the piles of racks.

Just carry them out? he asked. Smell of dust and mildew, smell of walnut husks. Smell of his childhood. If he closed his eyes, he could go right back, and no doubt this was what his mother was doing now. We have the same childhood, he said. Because of the smell of this room.

Not the same, she said. You have no idea. You can't imagine what it was like.

Fine, he said. Your specialness can't be touched. So where do you want the racks?

His eyes were adjusting and he could see them more clearly now, square wooden frames with mesh screens. Stacked like bricks, making a wall.

I'm only telling you the truth, she said. It was a different time. I'm not the enemy.

He clenched his teeth and made a growling sound and shook his arms. It was just what he felt.

You won't be able to do that to anyone else, she said. You treat me worse than you'd be allowed to treat any other person. I'm just about at the end of my patience.

Your patience? Galen asked. He grabbed a rack and stepped around the tractor, into the bright hot sun. His blood pounding. He walked twenty yards to the staging area and set the rack down in the dirt. He got on his knees and grabbed big dirt clods like the earth's own walnuts and set them in the rack. Dark crusted shapes already drier than the sun itself, and these would put the rack to good use.

The towels on his legs were too difficult to keep in place, so he let them fall. Bare legs and underwear, a green sweater and green boots. He passed her on the way back to the shed, kept his eyes on the ground. I haven't done anything to you, he hissed.

Like jousting, he thought. Tilting at each other, only a brief moment of contact. He stepped into darkness, grabbed a rack and set it on the ground, grabbed another and stacked it, grabbed another. They were heavy, made of wood, and he wasn't sure he could carry three at once, but he picked them up, his back washing out a bit, then recovering. He stumbled outside, his cheek pressed against wood, and tottered his way to the staging area.

His mother was removing all the dirt clods from the rack he had placed. Those aren't dry yet, he said. But she didn't say anything in return. Just knelt there in the dirt in her work pants and one of her father's old work shirts, sun hat and gloves, removing clods.

He set down the stack of three racks and headed back for more. He grabbed another three, brought them out into the sun. Then he had an idea.

He set all six racks next to each other in a long row, and he lay down on the racks, careful not to punch through any of the mesh screens. He made sure his butt and head and ankles were supported on the wooden edges. Another edge made a crease in his back.

Why do you do this to me? his mother asked. Her voice as quiet as a whisper.

Green Walnut needs to be dried, he said. And these are the drying racks. He tried to keep his eyes open, staring up into the midday sun. He was roasting in his sweater, and his bare legs and face would burn. He would stay out here the rest of the day. The wooden edges so hard across his back and neck he didn't know how he'd last even the next five minutes, but he was determined. It would be a meditation, and who knew what might lie on the other side.

All I've sacrificed for you for more than twenty years, his mother said in a low voice. Get up before Helen and Jennifer see you.

Galen could hear his aunt and cousin talking at the shed, coming this way. Why does it matter if they see? he asked. I'm just curious. I don't see why it would matter.

Just get up now.

No, he said. I'm staying here like this all day.

The sun so bright Galen couldn't see his mother, couldn't judge what might come next. But she only walked away.

He tried to relax into the hard wood, tried to let his flesh and bones find a soft way of fitting to the wood. The edges cutting into his butt were making his legs numb, and the edge across his back made breathing more difficult, but the one at his neck was the most urgent. He tried to exhale, stare at the sun, forget this existence, find something else.

You already look like jerky, his aunt said.

His thighs are white, Jennifer said.

True, his aunt said. And I guess they should match his face and neck.

Galen dizzy and blind, his eyes filled with flashes and spots, but he could hear the work on every side, a pointless task. The racks didn't need to be cleaned or oiled or maintained in any way, unless a screen was broken. But none of them knew how to repair a screen. If one was broken, they'd simply put that rack aside, in the pile directly behind the tractor, and not use it. So what was happening today was that they were taking all of the racks out of the shed and then putting them away again.

We're just going through the motions, Galen said.

What's that? his aunt asked.

Our whole lives, Galen said, just reenactments of a past that didn't really exist.

The past existed, his mother said. You just weren't there. You think anything that's not about you isn't real.

What about my father? Galen asked. Can you prove he's real? Can you narrow it down to the two or three men who are most likely, at least?

No answer to that. Never an answer to that. Only the sounds of their shoes in the dirt, the sounds of racks being picked up now, returned to the shed.

I have some other questions too, Galen said. I'm not finished.

But no one was listening to him, it seemed, and his back was so destroyed by now it hurt too much to speak. So he closed his eyes, saw bright pink with white tracers and solar flares, a world endlessly varied and explosive. His body spinning in the light. Face and thighs cooking, a stinging sensation. But he would stay here, he would see this out.

Pain itself an interesting meditation. On the surface, always frightening, and you wanted to run. Very hard not to move, very difficult, at least at first, to do nothing. Pain induced panic. But beneath the surface, the pain was a heavier thing, dull and uncomplicated. It could become a reliable focal point, a thing present and unshifting, better even than breath. And the great thing about these racks was that they distributed the pain throughout his body. He was afraid his neck and back might actually be damaged, and that was a part of pain, too, the fear of maiming, of losing permanently some part of the body. Even an insect didn't want that. No one wanted to lose a leg or an arm or the use of their back, and so as we approached this moment, we approached a kind of universal, and if we could look through that, and detach ourselves, we might see the void beyond the universals, some region of truth.

Stop thinking, Galen told himself. The thinking was a cheat, robbing him of the direct experience. And it's also bullshit, he said aloud. It's all bullshit. I'm just lying on a rack, and that's all.

His mother and aunt and cousin having high tea now. All sounds of their movement gone. Only the sounds of flies and bees on flight paths nearby, the dry landings of grasshoppers, an occasional car passing. The world in its immensity and such disappointing nothingness. Galen rolled over, off the racks, into the dirt. Just like that. No decision, just rolled over, and now it was gone, the entire experience, all wasted, and he was in the dirt again. Nothing learned, nothing gained.

alen tried to push up on his arms, but he felt broken. This sucks, he said. He lay facedown. The dirt scratching against his burned thighs hurt more than he would have guessed. The sweater an oven, a cocoon. A slick of sweat beneath, and he was thirsty. His face on fire.

His butt muscles were coming alive, blood rushing into his thighs, and his legs felt like hollow tubes, the muscle not attached to the bone. He pushed up onto his knees, then tried to stand, his legs like straws. Points of pain everywhere along their edges, the muscles unreachable, not responding. But he was able to take a step, and another. His back had been folded for too long, so he felt like he was leaning.

Almost got you, he said. You almost had to admit you're not really a body. Just a fake, an illusion, and I'm watching you reassemble now. All the clanking around to pull the dream back together.

He lurched his way around the shed to the fig tree where the other illusions were just finishing tea.

You look a little stiff, his aunt said, smiling. And suddenly he understood. His aunt hated him. It was instantly clear. He liked her, and he had thought she liked him, but now he could see that she hated his mother and hated him as her extension. Her smile all meanness.

Wow, Galen said. Holy shit.

What? Jennifer asked.

Nothing, he said.

We're finished now, his mother said. We'll be leaving to see Grandma in a few minutes.

Galen made his way carefully to the free chair and sat down. Cast iron, no cushion. His butt might fall back asleep. But it felt good to sit, and the shade was glorious. He closed his eyes to the smell of figs, a scent so rich it made a body of the air. Wow, he said. The figs.

Nearly ripe, his mother said. Another week at most. And she poured him a glass of orange juice. Here, she said. Even when she liked him least, she would provide for him. And this was the difference. His aunt would push him off the edge if she ever had the chance, but his mother would never do that.

Galen wrapped both hands around the cool glass of orange juice, and he wondered whether to drink it. He was thirsty, incredibly thirsty. And the orange juice would be delicious, cool and tangy, with a bit of pulp, and he loved the pulp. But he felt dizzy, the top of his head gone, a floating sensation, and he didn't want to lose that. He felt he was seeing everything more clearly now. The orange juice might stop all that. Too cold, too acidic, a jolt that would bring all his attention to his stomach, and he would no longer be floating free.

Freakazoid, Jennifer said.

Galen closed his eyes and tried to focus. What did he really want? He held the glass of orange juice in both hands and brought it closer, close enough to put his nose into the glass and smell the sweet fruit. He breathed the orange juice, in and out, in and out.

I can't watch, his mother said. We're leaving in five minutes.

Galen didn't like having the time pressure. That was changing the experience. An end was being enforced now, and that was going to fuck up everything. Damn it, he said.

Whoa, Jennifer said.

He didn't want her here. Or his aunt. He wanted to be alone with the orange juice.

And then he decided to just do it. He tilted the glass and tasted the juice, sweet and bitter and overpowering, and he held it in his mouth, refused to swallow.

Does Mikey like it? Jennifer asked.

He tried to forget her, tried to focus only on the sweet juice in his mouth, but it was impossible. He swallowed, and exactly what he had feared would happen did. The track all the way down to his stomach, and he felt the weight of his stomach, the caustic need, all of his awareness pulled downward, the top of his head no longer open. A stone sinking down, hitting bottom, stuck there now.

Thanks, he said. Thanks for fucking that up.

And what was that exactly? his aunt asked.

Nothing, he said.

Exactly, she said.

Galen opened his eyes, chugged the rest of the glass, then set it down on the table.

Welcome back, his aunt said. We are the humans.

You are empty shells, he said. Husks and nothing more. He got up and walked into the house, had to use a hand on the banister rail to get up the stairs.

He sat on the edge of his bed and bent over carefully to remove the sweater, drenched in sweat. Ow, he said. That really hurts. He could hardly breathe. He took off the boots, dropped his underwear, and stepped carefully into the shower. Took a cold one, for his legs, and even the cold water hurt. He dabbed himself carefully with a towel, then put aloe on his legs and face and neck. In the mirror, he looked unnaturally bright. The dark skin of his face had become bright pink beneath, a kind of secondary glow.

Galen, his mother yelled. We're waiting.

I'm coming, he yelled back. He put on clean underwear, a T-shirt, socks, and tennis shoes, walked carefully down the stairs.

Damn it, his mother said. Put on some pants. She was standing in the foyer with a hand on the doorknob. His aunt and cousin lounging in the sitting room.

My legs are burned.

Well of course they're burned. Put on some pants.

Fine, he said. He went back upstairs and found some old swim shorts that were too small and wouldn't cover more than a few inches of his thighs.

Cute, Jennifer said. I like that look. It would be even better if you pulled the white socks higher, up to your knees.

Shut up, Jennifer, his mother said.

I'm warning you, his aunt said.

Then his mother was out the door, and they all followed. He got in the backseat, and Jennifer slid in beside him, his aunt up front. He had a boner by the time they pulled out of the lane. Suburbia all around them, housing developments. Theirs was the only undeveloped farmland for miles. Ten acres of walnuts, a few acres for the house and lawn, a couple acres for the driveway. Everyone else bunched up in quarter-acre lots or smaller.

Newly paved streets, winding, with thin saplings planted all along. But soon enough they were in the old section, houses from the fifties. And the old shopping center.

They have wonderful pumpkin pies at Bel-Air, he said.

Stop, his mother said.

They really do make wonderful pies.

How about you give it a rest, Galen, his aunt said.

It's been so long since I've tasted pumpkin pie.

Only the sounds of the car after that. A throaty engine, a big 350 or something, his mother had told him once. She was trying to get him excited, perhaps thinking he would start changing the oil and such, saving her some money. But he didn't give a shit about cars. He didn't care about anything that other people cared about. He was not here to be a slave to houses and cars and jobs and marriage and kids and TV and all that crap.

He put his hand on his boner, squeezed it a bit, tight in the shorts. Jennifer staring out her side window. And then they were piling out of the car and he was trying to hide the boner by tucking it into his waistband and holding out the front of his T-shirt. Looked obvious, probably, and he couldn't think of a way to make his hands look natural, but he couldn't think of anything else to do, and his aunt and mother weren't looking at him anyway.

Suzie-Q, his grandmother said when they shuffled in. She just didn't look that old. It didn't make any sense that she was here. They were all waiting for her to die, but it might be a very long time. Twenty years or even longer. She was only seventy-one.

She hugged Galen's mother, and then she hugged Galen. A strong squeeze.

My handsome grandson, she said. Are you getting ready for school?

Not this fall, Galen mumbled. I'm deferring a year.

Well, she said. I think that's a good idea. We talked about that. Take a year off. See the world first.

Galen couldn't bear to look at his aunt or Jennifer. His grandmother squeezed him again and then finally let him go.

Come sit, his grandmother said. So nice of all of you to visit.

There was nowhere for them to sit. One chair in the corner, then the two beds with their curtains, the old woman with the wet eyes in one of them, smiling at Galen now.

Sit on my bed, his grandmother said. So they did that, which meant they were all facing outward, away from each other in a kind of ring, stiff backs like the half-buried rocks at Stonehenge, waiting. Galen's grandmother grabbed the chair from the corner and brought it over to sit.

Look at all of you, she said, smiling.

How are you, Mom? Galen's aunt asked.

Oh, I'm fine, she said. How long has it been since you last visited? Has it been a year? And is that Jennifer?

Of course that's Jennifer, his aunt snapped. And it's only been a month. Less than a month.

Suzie-Q visits me every day. And Galen, even though he's busy getting ready for school in the fall. She was smiling at him, that new and foreign face in her dentures, not the face he grew up with. Well, his grandmother said. Isn't this nice.

I'd like to talk with you, Mom, Galen's aunt said. About the trust, and about college for Jennifer. This will be her senior year of high school, and then she'll be going to college, so we need to make arrangements.

Oh, we have plenty of time for that.

I'd like to talk about it now, Mom.

It's maybe a little early, Galen's mother said. We could wait until later in the fall, couldn't we? Or even the winter.

Shut up, Suzie-Q.

Stop that, Helen. Don't talk to your sister like that. You've always been like that.

Galen's aunt took a deep breath and closed her eyes.

I thought there wasn't any money for college, Galen said. Is there money for college?

Oh, I don't have any money, his grandmother said.

That's right, Galen's mother said. There's only enough to pay for this good care home.

Galen's aunt was shaking her head, looking down. I hate this so much, she said. I hate this more than I could ever possibly say. Her fists were clenched in her lap. Lies all my life. Both of you. Only lies.

Stop it, Helen.

Because I've been so bad. Helen has said the truth, and we hate the truth, so we hate Helen.

Stop it, Galen's grandmother said again. You're just awful. You never stop.

That's right. I'm always the awful one. I'm the one who needs to be beaten after you've been beaten. But never Suzie-Q. Never little Suzie-Q. Suzie-Q helps us pretend that we're good.

Mom, we don't have to listen to this. I'll take you out to the garden. She stood up from the bed, walked over to her mother, and the two of them were out the door quickly.

Galen could hear his aunt's shaky breathing, furious. And she gets everything in the will. She gets *everything*.

What do you mean? Galen asked.

She hasn't told you?

No.

Your mother gets everything. You don't get anything. Jennifer doesn't get anything. I don't get anything. It all goes to your mother. But then your mother will give it to you in her will. So I guess you'll be fine in the end.

The three of them sat there, looking down, and then finally his aunt got up. I'll be at the car, she said.

Jennifer stood up and closed the plastic curtain around the bed. Stand up, she whispered. So Galen stood up. Now drop your shorts.

Galen did as he was told.

And your underwear.

So Galen was hanging there bare.

Get it up, she said.

Galen didn't feel any desire at all. After all that? he asked. That's impossible.

Jennifer lifted her skirt, and then she reached down and pulled her panties aside.

Wow, Galen said. Light blond hair, a few wisps of it, and she opened her lips with a finger so he could see pink. Oh, he said, and he could feel his boner rise back up, in small lurches until it was hard and ached and he stepped toward her. But then she dropped her skirt.

Stand sideways, she said. And put your hands behind your back.

Okay, he said.

I'm going to slap your dick, hard, and you can't move, and you can't make a sound.

What?

If you move or make a sound, you'll never see my pussy again.

Why are you doing this?

Hold still.

She swung hard with an open hand, and what he felt was an explosion of pain. He wanted to scream, but he swallowed it. He kept his hands behind his back and closed his eyes and could feel the tears. Then the hard slap again, and he was whimpering, shaking.

She leaned in close and whispered in his ear. How does that feel?

Why did you do that?

She reached down for his balls. Don't move, she whispered.

No, he said. Please.

But she squeezed, gradually tightening her grip, and he felt the pain rise up into his stomach, the nausea. Please, he gasped.

Jennifer let go, then slapped one of his burned thighs, hard, which made him want to howl. Don't forget, she said. And then she stepped away through the slit in the curtain and was gone.

Galen tried etheric surgery. Sitting on his bed, imagining a small golden hook dangling from his right hand, he swept the hand over his wounded dick and let the hook pull through and heal. Ideally, his left palm should be underneath, to help create an electromagnetic field for the healing, but it didn't seem right to just sit on his hand. There had to be some airspace for this to work. So he turned on his side and had his left hand out behind his bare butt and waved his right hand in front of his dick. Now his golden hook was hanging straight down, though. He had to free his mind from gravity. There was no reason the golden hook couldn't hang out to the side. It was etheric, after all. But his mind was just stuck on the hook hanging down. He couldn't relax properly into his breathing. And his dick hurt. It was red and puffy on one side, even when it was limp. And he had a small bruise at the base, as if the whole thing had been broken off at the stem. He was afraid a boner would hurt even worse.

He didn't understand how Jennifer could have done this. His balls were tender, too.

Galen closed his eyes and tried to imagine the hook. Swinging tightly to the side on a slim golden chain, and then he realized he had never imagined the chain before. Was it supposed to be on a chain, or just a hook out there by itself? And did he really need airspace? How did the ether work?

He tried to feel the healing, tried to let it happen, but it wasn't happening. He remembered a troubleshooting section in the book on etheric surgery. Something about reestablishing a field. So he held his palms still, one a few inches behind his butt and the other a few inches in front of his crotch, and he tried to feel the force field between them. He pushed them lightly toward each other, like fluffing cotton candy, felt the energy now in the center of his palms, could feel them pushing at each other.

Okay, he said.

And now he tried to feel the energy in his crotch, tried to feel the path of that energy from palm to palm as he pushed and fluffed. A kind of warmth, the ether something that was always lit and warm, a little crackly from electricity, but no, that wasn't right, it wasn't crackly. Just a smooth warmth and light, and now he was able to dip his right hand and swing the hook through this warmth. He could feel its tug, and it wasn't where he expected, not on his dick itself but deeper in his crotch at some base, and this was the beauty of etheric surgery. It could find the right places, the sources, and replenish those sources. It wasn't fooled by the surface of things. And the hook didn't need a chain. It was swinging out there on its own.

Galen exhaled deeply into the healing. Deeply and more deeply, sinking, the hook a kind of butterfly, fluttering inside him, and when he awoke, his mother was pounding at his door and his cheek was in a puddle of drool.

Uh, he said. Uh. He wasn't up to speech yet. He wiped his cheek on a fresh bit of pillowcase and rolled onto his back.

And stop locking the door, she yelled.

Uh, he said, and he could hear her steps down the stairs.

Galen felt like he was climbing out of a deep well. A late-afternoon nap could really knock him down.

He sat up on the edge of his bed, the world still swirling a bit. Remaking itself, the appearances all knitting together again. He put his palms out and tried to levitate a few inches in the air, right now, while the world was caught off guard, before it was fully solid again.

Come on, he said. He tried to get the ether to lift his butt, but gravity was gluing him down, and it was too late. The world had remade itself. He hadn't been quick enough. Fuck, he said. I have to be quicker.

He looked around for his underwear. Several pairs on the floor, maybe a dozen scattered around, and he couldn't remember which was the clean pair from this afternoon. So he just went for the closest and hoped that was right.

He pulled on his T-shirt and shorts, which stung, lathered his thighs with aloe, a cooling, wonderful relief, tied his shoes but still felt so groggy he lay back down.

Galen! his mother yelled.

So he sat up and stumbled over to the door, down the stairs to the dining room. She had set the table with candles, even though it wasn't dark out yet. Plates at either end of the long table, using the old Polish china with the edges painted in red and blue. A large round of sourdough bread in the middle of the table, filled with a white dip.

I fixed onion dip, she said.

He walked up close to it and looked down. White with brown streaks, the onions. Crackers on a wooden board, and vegetables cut up. Hunks of broccoli and cauliflower, whole carrots and slices of bell pepper.

I fixed a vegetarian meal for you, she said. Fresh vegetables, not even cooked.

Thanks, Mom, he said. This looks great. He grabbed his plate and filled it with veggies and crackers and a few hunks of sourdough bread, then spooned a mound of dip. He was famished. Wow, he said.

He sat down, and his mother looked pleased. Thanks, Mom, he said again. Then he dipped a hunk of broccoli and put it in his mouth. Creamy and delicious, and a good crunch in the broccoli. He closed his eyes and hummed as he ate. Only the best meals brought on the humming.

Food was a meditation, an opportunity not to be missed. He sat very tall, erect in his chair, his crown chakra open, and let the food thrum through his body. He kept his eyes closed and felt for his food with his hands, dipped his fingers in the luscious dip and sucked on them, breathed in the bread before he chewed, crunched away at the slices of bell pepper, so juicy and fresh.

I love this, he said.

Shall we take our plates to the fireplace? his mother asked.

Sure, he said. We haven't done that in a while. He piled more veggies on and they walked into the front room with the piano and high ceilings. Tucked inside, at the very center of the house, was an enormous hearth made of granite slabs from the Sierras, with rugs in front. Galen lay down, propped his elbow on a pillow, and kept eating. His mother lay down facing him.

Where are we? she asked. It was their game, from as far back as he could remember.

In mountains, he said. In front of larger mountains.

Mongolia, she said. Maybe Mongolia.

And we've ridden here across a wide plain.

Snow and winter, she said. The horses with blankets.

The plain had only hard tufts of grass, nothing for the horses to eat.

We're running from someone.

Or everyone.

Yes. His mother was excited, up on an elbow now, leaning in closer. Her eyes gray with flecks of gold, similar to the granite. Running from everyone. That's right. They don't understand us, and we're alone. We can't talk to anyone.

She was too close. He could feel her breath on his face. So he sat up. I need more dip, he said, and he grabbed his plate and went for the table. They hadn't played this game for months, and it seemed to him a strange game now. Sometimes they'd lie in front of the fireplace and whisper for hours. Inventing places and lives and telling secrets about people who didn't exist. All his life they'd done that, but it felt creepy now. He didn't know what it was. Maybe Jennifer calling him a mama's boy. Or maybe seeing Jennifer up close. But something to do with Jennifer. Maybe because his mother and Jennifer were the same in some ways, separated only by age. He didn't like to think about this. He was really creeping himself out.

Galen spooned more dip onto his plate and returned to the fireplace but this time sat on the wide stone front.

Are you enjoying your food? she asked. She was lying back on the rug, looking up at him.

Yes, he said, and he closed his eyes, focused on the chewing. The dip saltier than he had first noticed.

I'm glad, she said. I thought we'd have a nice treat since the terrible two aren't here.

Galen tried to keep his focus on a carrot and the way it crunched in his teeth. He could feel it sever, all that solidity cracked through in an instant, a clue to how one might get the world to slip for a moment. Removal from the world. Distance. That was what he needed. It was awful how quickly he could forget that.

It was so nasty of Helen to pick a fight right before our trip.

So like her. She'll never let things just be good. She's an unhappy person. She always has been.

What trip? Galen asked. He kept his eyes closed and tried to remain focused on his chewing.

We're going to the cabin tomorrow.

Tomorrow?

Galen. I've had the trunk of the car packed for two days now. We're leaving at eight.

Eight o'clock? Galen had his eyes open now. I hate getting up early.

It's just one day. It won't kill you.

But why? Why can't we leave at noon? It's only an hour and a half from here.

Galen.

Fine. Is Grandma coming?

Yes. Of course.

Is it true that everything goes to you in the will?

Who said that?

Helen.

Galen's mother sat up, grabbed her plate, and walked into the kitchen. I don't feel like talking about it, she said.

But Galen followed her in. And what about college? Is there money for college? Why was she asking for Jennifer?

His mother put her plate in the sink and ran the tap. Helen is in dreamland. She's always been there.

But there is some way that Grandma or the trust could pay for college?

She shut off the tap and rested her hands on the sink. Look, she said. There are things written in the trust. That money can be used for medical expenses, or education, or even a house. Helen's been trying for a house. She wants everything. But there's not enough money for that. Mom may live another ten years, and that rest home is expensive.

How much money is there?

Galen.

I'm serious. How much money is there? Galen could feel the anger like a wave of heat. It was amazing how quickly it could come. He was standing behind his mother, looking down at the back of her neck. He was only inches away.

Stop, she said, and she walked out the back door, but Galen followed her onto the lawn. Leave me alone, she said. She looked frightened, and he felt suddenly how small she was, how frail. She was backing away from him.

I could have gone to college four years ago, he hissed. That's what the trust is for. If it says it can be used for education, then that's what it's for. But you didn't tell me. Because you want to keep it all for yourself.

Stop, Galen. You don't understand. She was backing away toward the shed. She had her hands out, fending him off.

How much money is there? he yelled. How much fucking money?

Galen, you're scaring me.

He growled and grabbed her by the shoulders, hard, pushed her back against the wall of the shed.

Help! she screamed. Someone help me!

Galen let go. What the fuck, he said. I'm not going to hurt you. What the fuck are you thinking? That I'd actually hurt you? I'm just trying to find out the truth. How much money are you hiding from us?

Galen couldn't look at her. He walked back into the house and up to his room. He was shaking. He couldn't believe she had thought he would hurt her. As if he were some kind of monster.

n the morning, Galen couldn't shake the feeling that his mother was the enemy. All his life, maybe. It was hard to tell how far back. When had she turned against him, and why?

He hadn't been able to sleep. He'd wandered the orchard until some time past four. So getting up at seven was hell. He was a kind of ghost, but he didn't have the energy to try to use that in some way. Packing didn't make any sense. A mismatched bunch of clothing crammed into a duffel, and he put five new C batteries into his tape recorder, brought all his tapes. He brought the old spearfishing lance that had somehow become his, passed down from one of his mother's men. Packed his pocketknife and binoculars and hiking compass. Hid several issues of *Hustler* in his clothing, and also packed *Siddhartha*, *The Prophet*, and *Jonathan Livingston Seagull*.

You can't bring that, his mother said when he came downstairs with the lance.

I'm bringing it.

It won't fit.

I'll stick it out the window.

His mother was wearing an apron. She'd been making sandwiches, no doubt, probably up already for hours. Cabin trips were a very big deal for her. There's nothing to spear, she said.

Trout, he said.

The trout in that creek are six inches long, Galen. If you're lucky. And most of the water is less than a foot deep.

There are a few deeper holes.

You're not bringing it.

Then I'm not going.

She walked away into the kitchen and came back with a peanut butter and jelly sandwich. Damn you, she said, and she threw the sandwich at him. A soft puff against his chest and it fell to the floor, separated. Peanut butter facedown, strawberry jam up.

You throw like a girl, he said, and he picked up the sandwich, put it together, and started eating.

She stood in front of him and cried. Shoulders slumped, head down, her hair curled, and wearing that apron. She just stood there and cried.

Normally he'd feel tremendously guilty and give her a hug. Normally he'd want to make things up to her. But something had changed. He didn't like her. I don't know who you think your audience is, he finally said, and he carried his lance out to the car.

The mafia showed up as he was packing his things away. Jennifer wearing a pink sweatshirt with the hood up, looking sleepy. Hard to believe she'd been so vicious. She looked soft and edible.

The air wasn't too hot yet, but the sun was up and so bright Galen was squinting. He never saw this time of day. Everything pale, washed-out. No depth. A two-dimensional world, a cardboard cutout. The hedge and the walnut trees in the same vertical plane though they were a hundred feet apart. Galen reached out to try to fit his hand in the gap.

What are you doing? his aunt asked.

It looked for a second like I could touch where the hedge and trees meet.

Yeah, she said. I thought that was probably it. Maybe you should try again.

Galen put his hand down. His aunt made him feel like a stupid little boy, and he didn't like that feeling.

What's wrong? his aunt said. You were almost there. Go ahead and touch it.

Galen walked into the house, through the foyer and dining room into the kitchen. His mother was slumped in a kitchen chair. Can I help? he asked.

She didn't look up but pointed at a picnic basket on the table. A wicker basket covered by a red-checked cloth, another perfect idea, the dream of a picnic basket. Galen picked it up and walked out to the car.

Little Suzie-Q, his aunt said. I'd like to take a shit in that basket.

Galen felt protective of the basket now. He got in the backseat with it on his lap and his lance poking out the open window, a kind of guardian of old. Jennifer a few feet away, slouched against her door, trying to fall back asleep, and his aunt in the passenger seat, all of them waiting.

The car heating in the sun, and Galen's mother took her time. Walked slowly out, got in without a word, and drove them away down the hedge lane.

They make the most wonderful pumpkin pies, Galen mumbled as they passed Bel-Air.

No one responded. They really are the most wonderful pies, he said. The pumpkin especially.

Galen's grandmother was not ready for the trip. That was one thing about losing your memory. You could never be ready for anything.

Today? she asked. She looked frightened.

Yes, Mom.

But I haven't packed.

We packed your things last week. We have a suitcase set aside.

I need to go home, she said. I need to go home to gather my things.

We're going to the cabin, Mom.

I need to go home.

You love the cabin, Mom. We always have a wonderful time there. We go every summer. We use the old cast-iron stove, and you fix chicken and dumplings.

Why won't you take me home?

Galen's mother turned around, her back to her mother. I can't do this today, she said quietly. One of you will need to bring her to the car. Her suitcase is in the closet.

What are you doing? Galen's grandmother asked.

Galen's mother left the room then, and Galen looked at his aunt.

You come back here, Suzie-Q, Galen's grandmother said.

I don't even exist, Galen's aunt said. Ask her if I'm here, and you'll find out. Jennifer doesn't exist either. We're invisible. So it's all on you.

Grandma, Galen said. We get to go to the cabin. We'll have hot chocolate.

Where is your mother?

Galen walked over to her closet and took out the small suitcase. Looks like you're ready to go, he said. Mom's in the car.

She's in the car?

Yeah, we're going to the cabin.

Okay, she said, and just like that they walked out.

Galen's grandmother sat in front. Galen and the mafia in the back, Jennifer jammed in the middle. The feel of her thigh, plump and firm against his bony leg. He wanted her to be wearing shorts, but she wore sweatpants. If only the others could just disappear.

The day hot now, the air from the open windows getting hotter as they passed fields of dry yellow grass. Galen could feel a bead of sweat trickle down his chest, and Jennifer was in a panic suddenly to get rid of her sweatshirt. All elbows, Galen's aunt complaining, but Galen had a chance to see Jennifer's bare arm and armpit, the curve to her breast in only a tank top, so close to his mouth. He turned away, looked out the side window so his aunt wouldn't catch him.

The open windows at highway speed made it impossible to speak, and this was a relief to everyone, it seemed. Even his mother and aunt might get along if they could just live in a blast furnace. Words could only cause trouble. Galen enjoyed the peace, watched the landscape slip past, yellow grass dotted with oaks, the hills beginning to take shape, long curves of road climbing into pine trees, the gold rush country, the place of nostalgia for his grandmother who loved Hallmark cards and watched *Bonanza* on TV. Her perfect world was a small western town in which all words were sweet and empty.

Galen didn't know how his grandmother was possible. He had brought her into this existence to help him learn something, but how was her real life convincing? Could she really care about that TV ranch, with Hoss and all the other folk?

The smell of pines, the road wide, and the Buick floating and dipping. They rose higher into mountains, taller trees, more shade, and his mother pulled onto the shoulder. I'm just going to let it cool down a bit, she said. So we don't boil over.

They all piled out. Steep rock rising thirty feet from the side of the road. A mountainside dug and blasted. The air still hot despite the elevation and the shade. Galen walked over to the rock and scrabbled up a few feet to where he could lean against it, cool on his face and hands.

Rock brother, Jennifer said.

I'm touching another time, Galen said. When they cut into this mountain, they opened up another time. I wonder when it was.

The Freakazoic, Jennifer said. All the animals were skinny then and ran around doing random shit.

Helen laughed. Good one, Jennifer, she said.

You're not quiet enough to be at peace, Galen said. He closed his eyes and breathed in the rock, old smell. If all the world were illusion, only an old soul could have dreamed something so solid into existence. But what if the world were real, and only the people illusions, and the surface of things? The surface mutable, but not the core. Nothing Galen had read made any of this clear. It could be that this rock was real, and in that case it should be treated with a different kind of reverence. Galen breathed out a low note, deep in his throat, an ancient guttural song for the rock.

Oh please, his aunt said, but he ignored her. He repeated the low note, again and again, and then sang something up high, and then low again, and the song began to surge in him. His arms and face flat against the cool rock, and the rock was giving back an echo, very faint, but enough for him to hear up close. He was singing with the rock now.

So talented, he heard his grandmother say. My talented grandson. And this was disrupting his focus. Why wouldn't they all just vanish?

I can't stand it, his mother said. We're going. I don't care if the car overheats. Galen, get in the car.

Galen tried to hold on to the song and to the rock, tried to feel its spirit, but once his mother had decided, she wouldn't stop. There'd be no way to focus, so he gave up. Let his arms down and sighed and stepped carefully through scree to the road.

I was just getting somewhere, he said.

What a shame to lose that, his aunt said.

You have a lot of incarnations left, Galen said. You've only just started.

His aunt laughed, and kept laughing as they got in the car again. Jennifer had a few chuckles too, the laughter contagious.

Stop that, Galen's grandmother said, but they kept laughing, and his mother pulled onto the road again and there was the rushing of the air and their laughter that was entirely mean, not real laughter, no joy in it, and Galen looked out his side window and tried to ignore.

Exposed granite everywhere, the scale immense. Horsetail Falls up a tremendous gorge. The sheer face of Lover's Leap, granite pyramids and ridges scattered with pine, fir, and aspen, and the air cooler now. They rounded a bend, followed the river, turned off the highway onto a small bridge over a wide shallow pool where Galen had hunted trout from his earliest memories.

A forest service tract with small cabins on dirt roads bedded with pine needles. Dark and shady, the trees thick in here. Galen felt the excitement he'd always felt on arriving. Their cabin a small two-story with a steeply pitched roof. The walls in vertical slats of thick wood painted pale green, the storm shutters over the windows a dull burgundy. The wide deck and its thick wooden railing this same color, covered now with pine cones and needles.

We made it, Mom, Galen's mother said. We're at the cabin.

We need to turn on the water, Galen's grandmother said. She was already opening her door and stepping out.

That's right, Mom. You remember.

Of course I remember.

They all got out and stretched, and Galen set the picnic basket on top of the car, leaned his lance against a pine tree. His grandmother already heading up the hill.

Go with her, Galen, his mother said. So he hoofed it after her, trying to catch up. Around the deck and past the small toolshed. She was wearing pale green pants the color of the cabin, a brown blouse, stepping smartly. She stopped and bent down at exactly the right spot, reached into the bushes, removed a loose piece of bark, and turned the faucet that was hidden there.

You knew right where that was, Galen said.

Of course I did. Go around front and open the spigot. Let the water run until it's clear.

Aye, aye, he said, and walked back down.

Where's Mom? his mother asked.

She asked me to turn on the spigot.

Don't leave her alone.

I'm turning on the spigot. He stepped past the car to the pine tree he'd leaned his lance against. A tall spigot hiding behind it, and he turned it all the way open and water rushed out, a bit dark at first but then clearing. He grabbed some with his palm, icy cold, and had a drink. Nice, he said. Then he turned the spigot off.

His mother unlocking the storm door, his grandmother giving directions. The mafia standing by on the deck, watching with their arms folded. Galen felt almost bad for them for a moment, always on the sidelines. But that was just the order of things. Galen and his mother were first, and they were second, and that was just the way it was. It couldn't be changed.

Galen grabbed his duffel from the trunk. The cabin open now, and his mother unhooking storm shutters over the windows, but his grandmother had wandered inside. He followed her into darkness.

A closed-in smell, an entire winter. Smoke more than anything else, from the cast-iron stove in the kitchen. But other smells, also, of old wood and blankets, newspapers and kindling, mothballs. He loved this place, loved it more than any other.

His grandmother always went to the kitchen first. Galen followed, just in time to see the light come in as his mother opened the storm shutters from outside. His grandmother standing at the stove with her hands resting on it, looking down, remembering? He watched her being made in the pale light, created for the first time.

Her face older than he had realized, lines in arcs down her cheeks. Her eyes hooded. She was leaning over the stove as if she might collapse upon it, but then she straightened up and ran her palms over the round iron plates. She turned her face away.

Galen felt he was intruding, so he ducked up the narrow staircase, dragging his duffel. Darkness again, and he put his hand out to find one slim bed and then the other, stepped into the small aisle between and swung his duffel onto the bed on the left. Then he lay down, the bumpy old mattress. This was where he could think. He'd lain right here for hours each summer, throughout his life, dreaming of what might be. It was here that everything could be reviewed and here that who he was could be known. Only this place right here.

The bad thing, of course, was that it had to be shared with his mother. Galen could hear his mother and aunt arguing below about the sleeping arrangements, so he felt in the duffel for his tape recorder and earphones and listened to Kitaro's *Silk Road*.

He could feel his breathing calm and all the stress leave his body. So much stress, always more than he was aware of until he washed up on Kitaro's shore. Here he could spread his arms wide and he could fly.

But then the light turned on. His mother, wrecking everything. I'm listening to Kitaro, he hissed.

I can't fight everybody, she said. I don't have the energy.

Galen reached over and turned off the lamp, but she turned it on again. She had a small suitcase on the floor and was moving her clothing into the drawers of the narrow dresser between their beds. We're having our picnic now, she said. Up at the big rock.

I'm not hungry.

Then you'll just watch us eat.

Galen hit rewind, the old recorder squealing. He needed a Walkman. But of course there was no money for a Walkman. He hit play and was back on the Silk Road, his eyes closed.

Galen relaxed again, waited for the light to turn off and his mother to leave, and lying here in the cabin on this old mattress in the dark he had the sense that he was destined for something. The shape of his life might include greatness of some sort, though it was too early to tell what that might be. He could feel the expansiveness of his spirit, the way it emanated from his chest and filled the entire room. But he couldn't really focus, because they were all walking up to the big rock now, and that was a nagging that pulled at him. He should just not go, but somehow it was not possible to not go. His mother a constant disruption, a tearing in the fabric of space and time. There could be no peace when she was near.

Galen slammed the stop button on the recorder and took off the earphones. Then down the steep stairs.

The big metal stew pot on the stove, and that was one thing Galen was looking forward to, the chicken and dumplings. That was a meal he would eat, a break each year from being a vegetarian.

He stood at the stove like his grandmother had, placed his hands where hers had been, wondered what she'd been thinking or re-membering. Her own psychic space, where all the different times came together. Her children young, her husband still alive, her mind still intact. Could she remember that? Can a broken mind remember when it was well?

Galen turned his head away, as his grandmother had done, and ran his hands over the round cast-iron burners that could be lifted to poke at the coals. Black iron with chrome along the edges. The chrome tarnished but still beautiful, ornate curls and leaf patterns. A high back around a black stovepipe. The heft and solidity of the thing. Its presence in this small room and in their lives. Manifested by us, Galen said, his voice low. Brought into this incarnation as a signpost, a gathering point. I honor you, old stove. He closed his eyes and, ducking his head slightly, bowing, breathed out a long exhale.

The big rock another gathering point. He didn't want to see his family, but he did want to see the rock again, so he stepped out the back door, across the deck and into pine needles, then up the path to the meadow. Only a sprinkle of grass, bright green shoots in an open clearing, sunny. A break from the shade of the trees. And partway up the meadow, tucked into the left side, a large boulder taller than a person, very wide and set into the ground. A kind of lumpy pancake in layers of granite. Moss-covered in the lower shaded parts, the alcoves and overhangs. A few small ferns. Spotted with yellow blooms of lichen on top. Old skin of the rock. Jennifer perched in the place he liked to sit. She knew that was his place.

His aunt and mother and grandmother all sitting on the ground, leaning back against the rock. Mother and grandmother on one side of the picnic basket, aunt on the other. Red-checked cloth set out with peanut butter and jelly sandwiches, deviled eggs, pickles, potato chips.

My handsome grandson.

Galen tried to smile but found his face unresponsive.

Have a deviled egg, she said, as if she'd made them herself.

Thank you, Grandma, he said, and picked up a deviled egg, then climbed the rock to sit beside Jennifer. She'd taken the one smooth saddle in the top, the natural seat. She was staring ahead into space, crunching potato chips.

Galen closed his eyes and tried to calm, but he could hear everyone chewing. His mother biting into a dill pickle, unbelievably loud, his aunt chugging some orange soda, his grandmother gumming away at her sandwich making little smacking sounds. Jennifer with her potato chips that sounded like trees splitting. He hated human chewing and swallowing. He tried to focus on bees circling around in the wildflowers, and the sound of the creek not far away, a light breeze in the treetops farther up the hill, or even the cars passing on the highway, muffled by the forest. But all he could really hear were the wet sounds of tongues and gums and throats.

Listen to all of you, he said. All the chewing and swallowing.

None of the sounds stopped or even paused. We're eating, his mother finally said.

Jennifer took a bite of her sandwich and then gummed and smacked it as loudly as she could. She was smiling, watching him. She opened her mouth to show him the chewed-up mush.

Galen looked down at his deviled egg. The white a kind of cup for a bright yellow whip of goo, sprinkled with paprika. He sniffed it, and his stomach lurched. It had the smell of barnyard, and he was having to listen to the animals all around him.

Animals, he said. You sound like a bunch of animals.

Galen, his grandmother said.

Sorry. Galen climbed down and walked into the center of the clearing. He found a stick and dug a small hole, nestled the deviled egg inside, and covered it with earth. Grow, he said. Grow more deviled eggs.

He stretched his arms and tried to feel this open meadow and cool air, this familiar space. He gave a little yelp to see if there'd be an echo, but nothing came back. He could still hear their chewing, even from thirty feet away.

I'm going to the creek, he said. He tromped down through

the small trees at the side of the cabin, grabbed his lance from the tree at the spigot, and soon stood at the bank where he had stood every year. Slim shadows flitting away under rocks and overhangs. The trout.

Hard to tell how the trout knew his intentions, but they knew. Whenever he appeared, they were in the wide, shallow section, in less than a foot of clear water over a mottled bed of stones orange, green, dark blue, and brown. A kind of camouflage, but the trout knew. They knew the camouflage wasn't good enough and they instantly disappeared into the faster water, narrow chutes of white between larger stones and deadfall. Hidden pockets, caves and ledges. Places Galen couldn't see or reach.

For years, Galen had tried with various temptations: salmon eggs, bacon, corn, lures, and flies. He'd never caught a single fish. But this year was going to be different. This year he had brought the lance. He didn't have a spear point, so he'd duct-taped a ring of nails on the end, a dozen small stabbers. And he was going to sneak up on them from downstream, so they wouldn't smell him.

Through the trees, a larger pool that was a little deeper, almost two feet. This would be his entry point. He approached the pool carefully, but as soon as he was at the bank, the little shadows took off.

Run for your lives, he said. Papa's coming in this time.

He stripped at the bank and stepped in with one foot, then stepped quickly out. Holy shit, he said. The water was unbelievably cold. But he stepped in again, both feet, his ankles already in a dull ache, and went down on his hands and knees.

Oh, he said. Oh this is cold. But he eased forward, slipping his belly and chest in, and went under. His arms waving frantically underwater, the lance dropped. Trying to warm up, kicking his thighs in place, treading with his arms, banging his knees and feet and elbows on the stones as he thrashed. Nowhere to go in this small pool, but he had to warm up, had to move. He opened his eyes and they stung in the cold. He could feel the exact shape of his eyeballs, hard little lumps freezing in their sockets. He needed a mask and snorkel. He had to come up for air, and then he submerged again, smooth stones a few inches from his face, dappled light making a confusion of color. Everything suddenly larger, magnified.

A different world underwater. Galen's hands giant, his skin a tight sack holding his vital mush, his precious bit of warmth. He was a planet moving in a cold, weightless vacuum. Airless, impersonal, with a different relation to light. A thin membrane all that was keeping him alive.

He picked up the lance, heard it scrape against rock, sound magnified. Life on land a lesser life, everything muted, made small and dull. He looked around at stone and sand, root and dark earth along the bank, all of it expanded and luminous. The sunlight shifting and rippling, washing over in bands.

He had to come up again for air, his chest tight, and then he submerged and tried to relax, use less oxygen. The trout were all around him. If he could calm enough, he would feel their movement. Trout brothers, he thought. I am here with you now.

They were all in rocking chairs on the front deck.

He's a chameleon, Jennifer said. He's all white now. What happened to the red?

What did you do? his mother asked.

Fishing, he said, but his voice came out hollow and shaky. His teeth were chattering. He was careful up the porch steps, set his lance beside the door. He felt bony.

I guess we'll be feasting on trout tonight, then, his aunt said, and Jennifer laughed.

Today was just to figure out where they're at, Galen said.

They're in the creek.

Stop, his mother said.

That's okay, Galen said. I saw the creek today in a way you've never seen it, Helen. You have no idea what the creek is.

I've only been coming here my whole life.

That's the problem. Your whole life you've been only half waking.

Honestly, she said. What are you going to do when you have to go out into the real world?

The way you've done? Don't you live in a crap apartment paid for by Grandma? He was still having trouble getting the words out, his chest hollow. He really needed to warm up. I'm taking a bath, he said.

You'll have to turn on the water heater, his mother said. Takes about twenty minutes to warm up.

Fuck, he said. I'm really cold.

Galen, his grandmother said.

Sorry.

Are we leaving today? his grandmother asked. She looked suddenly worried.

No, Mom, Galen's mother said. We just got here. We have plenty of time.

Oh, she said, and settled back in her chair. I hate it when I can't remember.

Galen stepped inside and ran into the hide-a-bed. Can't you wait and put out the bed at night? he yelled.

You entitled little shit, his aunt yelled back.

Helen. It was a chorus from his mother and grandmother.

Galen climbed over the bed. In the bathroom, he flicked the switch for the water heater, closed the door and slumped against it and felt so sad suddenly. He'd never fought with his aunt, never in his life. The best of his early memories were with her, in fact. An inflatable pool on his grandparents' lawn, and she ran around the edge of it dragging him by the arms, making a whirlpool. Her laughter then always generous and real. He didn't know what had happened. Some mistake, something that shifted the wrong way in the last couple days. She'd made comments before, but he'd thought they were just in fun.

Galen didn't understand how lives were supposed to overlap. He had brought each of these people into this incarnation to teach him a specific lesson. But if his aunt had a spirit or a soul, too, then she had her own lessons to learn, and how did all of this line up? How could it be synchronized?

Maybe a person could be put on pause. His aunt still angry about her childhood. She hadn't realized yet that memory was only an illusion. Maybe you could remain stuck forever if you refused to learn a particular lesson. But she hadn't seemed angry before. Maybe it was Jennifer growing older. Maybe that was the difference. She was fighting for Jennifer now. In his earliest memories of his aunt, Jennifer didn't yet exist.

Galen's T-shirt and shorts were damp. He hadn't had a towel at the creek. His skin rough with goose bumps, shivering.

His grandmother, unable to remember anything, was definitely on pause. Someone taking a break from the game. Then there was the big question of what the game was even about. Why were we all trying to learn lessons? Galen knew it was so we'd finally be without attachment, but why did attachment ever have to exist in the first place?

Twenty minutes was a very long time. He stood and took off his damp shirt and shorts, grabbed a dry towel and rubbed himself with it, tried to get some heat through friction. The ceiling sagging in here, long planks hanging low in the center, a single bare bulb for light. This room an addition, not the original cabin, so apparently the old-timers didn't need baths. Maybe they just washed in the creek. They had all been tougher in the past. Though of course the past didn't really exist. History another illusion. It meant only what we made of it now.

Galen checked the tap a few times, and finally it was hot enough to run the bath. He sat in the tub while it filled, the most delicious heat. It was possible, of course, that he was the only real person here, the only one with a spirit or soul. It could be that each soul lived in a mirror-land with no one else around.

Galen dozed in the tub, sleepy from the heat, but then Jennifer was banging at the door. I'm next, she said. Hurry up. I want a bath before dinner.

So Galen rose and dried, careful on his thighs, which were hot and red again, and walked out in a towel.

I can see your ribs, Jennifer said. Even in your back. That's gross.

This is only a shell, Galen said. It doesn't matter.

We'll see, Jennifer said. She had her hair up and was already wrapped in a towel.

Galen went upstairs and wondered what that meant. His aunt and mother and grandmother all on the porch still. They hadn't started dinner yet, so it would be a while. He slipped under the covers and grabbed the *Hustler* from his duffel. He had to be careful not to come, in case she was planning a visit.

In the *Hustler*, the man was dressed as a musketeer, with a long feather in his hat. He was taking a break from his duties, and he had met several women who were short on clothing. The photo shoot was like a bad school play, but it didn't matter. Galen felt turned on anyway.

He was listening for anyone coming up the stairs, and finally that stressed him out too much, so he put the magazine away and waited.

Samsara, attachment to the world. Sexual desire was the worst of it. A need he could feel in his spine, all the way up his back and neck, connecting to his mouth. It was crazy, absolutely crazy, and it made time crawl. Only a eunuch could feel peace. Neutered. That was the fastest path to enlightenment.

He didn't really believe Jennifer would visit, but she did. She came up the steps and he turned on the bedside lamp. She was holding a deck of cards, wearing a skirt and T-shirt. I told them we're playing cards before dinner, she said.

She sat on his mother's bed and dealt pinochle hands on the bedside table. Her skirt was short, and Galen couldn't help trying to peek. He was embarrassed.

It's okay, she said, spreading her knees. You can look.

She wasn't wearing anything underneath.

We have a few rules, she said. One is that you can only do what I say. The other is that you can't make any sound. And of course you can't tell anyone.

Yes, he said.

She smiled. Look at you. You're so desperate. Twenty-two, and you've never had any pussy.

Have you had sex?

Of course, she said. Everyone has. Except you. Now lie back, and scoot down a bit.

He pulled the covers aside.

No, she said. Keep the covers on. And if anyone comes up the stairs, sit up quick and grab your pinochle hand.

Okay, he said. But what are we doing?

She climbed onto the mattress with her knees on either side of his head, then spread her knees and lowered down just above his face.

Wow, he said. She looked better than the women in the magazine, younger. So perfect, he said. So beautiful.

Don't make any sound.

Can I touch?

You can.

He felt the inside of her thigh with his cheek, with his nose. So soft and warm.

Use your whiskers, she said, so he ran the edge of his jaw along her thigh.

I like that, she said. Turn your face to the side and hold still.

He did as he was told, and felt her wet lips on his cheek.

Sandpaper, she said. I like that.

Galen felt a little annoyed, because he couldn't see with his head turned to the side. She was humping his jaw, which was kind of like she was having sex without him. He turned his face toward her but she pushed him back down, a hand on his forehead, and kept humping his jaw. He didn't like this at all. The whole side of his face was wet.

Okay, she said finally. She pulled his face upright and sat on it. You can lick.

Galen could hardly breathe. He moved his tongue around, but it didn't seem to matter much what he did. She moved up higher so that his nose was inside her, and she humped his nose. It didn't seem like his tongue was even on her pussy anymore. It was lower than that.

Lick my ass, she whispered, and he realized that was what he was doing.

I like that, she moaned. I like that. She sped up, bucking harder against his nose, which was locked into a kind of groove, and he just kept licking.

Galen couldn't hear well, the way she was humping his head down into the pillow in heavy swings, and he worried about someone coming up the stairs. The bed was probably knocking against the wall by now.

He was breathing through his mouth, and having to swallow. He felt like he was drowning. His entire face and forehead a slick.

I like that, she kept saying. She grabbed the back of his head with a hand and pulled him in closer. Shake your head as you do it, she said. So he shook his head back and forth as he licked.

Ooh, she said. Yeah. Keep licking.

He realized he had slowed down a bit with his tongue. It was hard to do it all at once: breathing, licking, shaking his head back and forth, trying to keep his whiskers in play.

Her thighs tensed, and she pulled his face up harder and slowed down. He could feel her trembling. She pushed into him hard enough once more to break off his nose, and then she was jerking in place.

Aah, she was saying. Aah. She rose off of his face and had a few more jerks. The muscles in her thighs, the soft lines, the beautiful pink. He couldn't believe he was seeing this. He'd lost his boner at first, but he had it back now, and he couldn't wait to put it in.

She climbed off, and he turned to the side to wipe his face on the sheet. Even his hair was wet.

Wow, he said.

She had her skirt back down and sat on his mother's bed. He pulled his sheet and blanket back, and she looked at his boner. Sorry, she said. I'm done.

What?

You can't have everything at once.

But I didn't get anything.

So entitled. My mother's right about you. You got my pussy, which is more than you deserve. Do you know how many boys at school would kill just to see my pussy?

Can I just look at it while I jack off, then?

No. I'm done. Pick up your pinochle hand.

Fuck, Galen said.

Don't be a baby.

Galen felt very angry suddenly. But he didn't want to say the wrong thing. So he sat against the wall, propped on his pillow, and picked up his cards.

There you go, she said. And you might want to wash your face before dinner.

Dinner was not chicken and dumplings. That would come later, when it could cook all day in the stew pot. Dinner tonight was a tuna casserole. A jar of mayonnaise, several large cans of tuna, a large bag of potato chips, and squares of American cheese on top.

You've really gone all out, Galen said.

Galen's mother was just setting the casserole on a hot pad in the center of the small table. The kitchen was tiny, and they were all elbow to elbow.

You've used an entire bag of potato chips, Galen said. Do you have any idea how much salt that is?

He was already starting to sweat, the cast-iron stove emanating incredible heat. They had the windows and back door open, but that wasn't enough.

Maybe it's time to throw away the white-trash cookbook, Galen said.

His mother grabbed his upper arm hard, pinching the skin, and yanked him out of his seat.

Suzie-Q, his grandmother said, and his mother let go. He sat back down.

Are we white trash? he asked. I'm never going to college, and none of us have jobs, and here we are out in the woods. Next thing you know, I'll be sleeping with my cousin.

Stop, Helen said.

Jennifer narrowed her eyes and then looked down at her plate. Maybe this was how he could have some power over her. Maybe she needed everything kept a secret more than he did.

This isn't you, Galen, his grandmother said. Your grandfather designed a bridge in Sacramento. You're a Schumacher, and you can always be proud of that.

Sorry, Grandma.

A pile of mush on everyone's plate, the wilted potato chips golden and oily.

Men are the problem, Helen said. First Dad and now you.

You won't talk to my son that way, Galen's mother said.

Weren't you just trying to rip his arm off?

He's not like Dad.

But I thought Dad was perfect. I thought he drank lemonade and had lovely lunches under the fig tree. Isn't it good to be like Dad? What happened to that whole story?

Your father was a good man, Galen's grandmother said. He worked hard all his life.

Yeah, we know, Helen said.

No you don't. You don't seem to understand. He provided for all of us.

I would rather not have been born, Helen said. Seriously. I would rather have skipped the entire miserable fuck-job of a life this has been.

Helen.

I'm serious. And I'm not putting up with your lies anymore. Why are you giving everything to Suzie? Why are you giving nothing to me, and nothing to Jennifer? I want to know, Mom.

Wow, Galen said. You can kick some ass when you get on a roll.

Galen's aunt punched him in the shoulder, hard. She punched him again, looking him right in the eyes, pure hatred, and punched him again. He tried to block, but she was fast, and she hit hard.

And then the strangest thing happened. Everyone looked away. No one said or did anything in response to the fact that his aunt had just punched him. His grandmother was humming to herself, looking down at her lap, and his mother was eating. Jennifer had crossed her arms and was looking down also. His aunt had gone back to eating. And what Galen realized was that this was the first time he'd been punched, but everyone else in this room must have been punched many times before. Or in his mother's case, maybe she had only been a witness to it, but a witness many times.

Galen's shoulder was throbbing, but he served himself some tuna casserole and tried to eat a couple bites. The sound of the fire in the stove, popping of coals. The sounds of chewing and swallowing, wet and amplified. The taste of salt.

Well, he said. I guess this is who we are.

Would you like some more casserole, Mom? his mother asked.

Thank you, yes. This is very good.

Galen's mother made a show of serving the casserole, raising the spoon high. Tomorrow we'll have your chicken and dumplings, Mom. That will be such a treat.

Galen could see his mother was the reconstructor of worlds. That was her role. When all fell apart, she stepped in and made time move again.

Tomorrow we can take a walk down at Camp Sacramento, she said.

Oh, that will be nice, his grandmother said.

I'm still waiting for an answer, Mom, Helen said.

Would you like some wine, Mom? Galen's mother asked.

Yes please.

Galen's mother stood and turned to the counter beside the stove. There was no space in this room. The five of them bunched around three sides of a tiny old table that was built into the wall, covered in a yellow plastic tablecloth. The walls uneven planks painted white. A single bare bulb with a chain. The floor a faded brown linoleum. The stove like a furnace. All their faces wet with sweat.

Galen's mother opened a bottle of white wine, Riesling, and the smell brought Galen instantly back. She poured glasses for herself and her mother and didn't offer to anyone else. The two of them drank and ate while Galen and the mafia watched, and Galen wondered why they were all together here.

What's the point of trying to be a family? he asked. Why are we doing it?

Galen's mother sighed and downed the rest of her glass, then refilled it. Galen's grandmother was staring at her own wine with a kind of wonder. She had rested it, nearly empty, on the table, just beyond her plate. The stem between two fingers, she was swirling it gently, her hand facing downward, open, as if she were waving her palm over something, as if the table were a looking glass and the wine upon it a kind of golden key. She looked mesmerized, her blue eyes wet and large, her lips moving slightly, as if she were reciting some invocation, something from long ago, something none of the rest of them would understand. She seemed about to announce something, and this was what kept the rest of them silent.

The bare bulb and its harsh light made it seem that if you removed his grandmother, you'd have to cut her from the fabric of the world and there'd be a hole left. Each of them felt that way to Galen, as if all were two-dimensional, flattened, and lodged in place. Jennifer with her arms still folded, looking down, unmoving, stationary. His mother with deeper lines around her mouth than he had noticed before, as if her lips were separate from the rest of her face, something added. Her eyes buried in sockets too large. The waves of her hair something sculpted and not attached. She looked fabricated, put together in pieces, invented.

Galen felt the unreality of her, felt it for the first time as something immediate and undeniable. She raised her glass again to her lips, but even that movement was jointed. The world put together with some kind of ratcheting action, each piece pulled into place under tension, all of it threatening to snap.

Galen wanted to leave. He wanted to get away from this table. This table felt extremely dangerous. He understood now that what held his family together was violence. But he was locked here, glued in place, unable to move. He could only watch, and the only movement was his mother's glass, and his grandmother's glass and palm moving in its slow circles, and the wavering of the light.

Galen read Kahlil Gibran's *The Prophet*, his most precious book, the one he studied when his attachment to the world became too much.

Your children are not your children.
They are the sons and daughters of Life's longing for itself.
They come through you but not from you,
And though they are with you yet they belong not to you.

Galen knew this to be true. He was greater than his mother, meant for more. She needed to understand that she had no claim over him. Or the illusion of her needed to understand that, or he needed to understand that the illusion of her had no hold over him, or something. It was all confusing. In any case, he needed to break her attachment to him, because she was holding him back. And his aunt needed to understand that she was free from her parents, that her life was her own. If only everyone could understand Gibran, there could be so much less suffering.

It was difficult to be in a family of younger souls. Galen was an old soul, nearing transcendence, learning his last and most difficult lessons, his final disengagements from family, but the rest of them were just beginning. They didn't know, even, that they were on the road. They didn't know the road existed, and it was tiring to try to wake them up and pull them along. It was a kind of service Galen was having to perform, a selflessness that was also one of the final lessons. At the moment, though, he didn't feel up to the task.

He rested *The Prophet* on his chest and looked around the small room in lamplight. The slanted ceiling, exposed wood, the vertical planks of the walls, painted dark brown. He wondered whether he might be a prophet, too. Perhaps that was his role.

Jesus had been a prophet. An ordinary man, a carpenter, but an old soul who was willing to help others see.

Galen loved this room, a place to remember who he was. It was easy to forget during the rest of the year as samsara worked away at him. But the room felt too small right now. Galen felt on the edge of learning something. He felt his soul expanding.

So he got out of bed, dressed in jeans and a sweatshirt and boots, since it would be cold outside, the mountains always cold at night. He tried to sneak down the stairs, but they were loud and creaking, and he didn't know which way to turn. If he went to the left, he'd have to pass his aunt and Jennifer to get out the front door. If he went right, he'd have to pass his mother and grandmother sitting at the kitchen table. He didn't want to go either way. He wanted a third door, but that's exactly what life never provided, and perhaps it was a good thing. This is how we were confronted, how we were forced to learn our lessons.

Galen went left, because he couldn't bear to be in that kitchen again with his mother and grandmother.

Jennifer and Helen on the hide-a-bed, leaning back awkwardly. There was a big gap between the mattress and back, so it was never possible to prop against pillows. They'd be getting kinks in their necks.

Let me guess, Helen said. You're being called by Father Granite to sing the pebbles into bigger rocks?

Galen ignored her and stepped outside. Down the steps quickly and into the dirt road, the pine needles. Clear, cold air, the smell of wood smoke, everything traced in moonlight.

"You shall see Him smiling in flowers, then rising and waving His hands in trees." Gibran was right. Galen needed only to learn how to look, how to feel. The pattern of moonlight through the trees. Everything around him a presence and a sign. The bodhisattva in all things. The Buddha in each rock and tree. Each pine needle better than a church.

Galen stopped and felt his connection to the ground, took off his boots and socks, concentrated on becoming lighter. Let the energy of the earth come up through his soles. He stepped forward again but tried to let it happen unplanned, tried to move authentically, tried to walk softly but not think about walking softly. Authentic Movement was something he was just learning about. There was a New Age bookstore near his grandparents' house, where he had spent most of his years after high school, but they'd told him not to come back, called him a stalker when all he'd been doing was aligning his aura with a young woman who worked there. She was a younger soul, lovely but afraid, unable to see. He had been trying to help her. The alignment worked best when he stood close behind her and put his arms out, but she didn't like that. The whole thing made him angry still, something he was trying to let go of. They were letting him order books by mail now, and the one on Authentic Movement was his most recent, letting the body find its own way, letting it speak back, learning from it, releasing attachment to self and past and anger, welcoming the connections to earth and air.

Galen's neck was slumped, and he could feel his lips heavy, like a frog's. For some reason, that always happened when he tried to concentrate, and it was distracting. Why was he even aware of his own lips? He wanted to be focusing on his movement.

He held his arms out, palms up, opened himself to the universe. Tried to let the movement happen, but somehow that just slowed him down and made his hips feel locked. So he tried a different stride, tried to walk the way he had over coals, more purposeful, longer strides. Only one workshop, one evening, and he had missed most of the talk because he'd agreed to tend the fire as a way to reduce how much he had to pay. Always having to beg his mother for money. A large bonfire, and it burned his face as the others talked about fear and using your fear as a counselor. He heard bits of it. Then he raked the coals into a bed fifteen feet long and three feet wide, the hot red embers and his face stinging.

Everyone gathered on the lawn in a ring around the coals, the grass cool and damp but the coals glowing. Galen felt afraid, but he was buoyed by the chanting around him, everyone with their arms out and palms up. Then they crossed the coals, one by one. Many of them jerked, a little hop after a few steps, burned. But some just crunched their way across.

When it was Galen's turn finally, at the end, he felt the most beautiful faith, a sudden rush of knowing that the universe would take care of him, a feeling that his fear had become something else more powerful, more pure, and he walked across with only a curiosity. He could feel the coals crushing under his feet, could feel their heat, even. He could feel each piece of wood, how fragile it was, how the fire was a kind of net that had pulled the substance from the wood, and he didn't burn. He walked across and was on the lawn again and felt he had received a great gift.

He helped clean up afterward, and he watched the woman who

ran the workshop tend to her feet. He hadn't seen her jerk or hop as she crossed, but the bottoms of both her feet were outrageously burned, long puffed areas of red skin like on a hot dog. She applied a white cream, then wrapped in bandages and stepped into large slippers. She popped a Vicodin.

What? she asked, and he didn't know what to say. She was making probably $20,000 in an evening, so that was perhaps the motivation, and he felt cheated.

Walking now on the pine needles, though, he tried to remember what he had felt as he'd crossed the coals, because something about that had been real. Something had happened, and there was no reason he couldn't enter that space again.

He tried to feel himself strung like a hammock between earth and moon. Wavering and catching the ethereal breeze, the wind from the shadow world. His body almost a tuning fork. His bare feet heavier on the road than he would have liked, so he tried to release them, tried to let them not carry any weight. He could feel sharp pricks from stones and needles, and he tried to ignore that, too. Ceremonial steps, a smooth movement, and he realized he was being pulled toward the wide, shallow water near the bridge, the open pool. He was being drawn there, and he didn't yet know why, but he was following that.

The road a corridor, laced in moonlight and shadow. A journey. He kept his eyes half lidded, tried to see without looking. Felt the energy gathering. His crown chakra wide open.

He chanted. *Heya hey hey, ya eh oh ee, ya eh oh ee, heya heya hey hey hey hey how.* A song he had learned once in a sweat lodge, a beautiful song, meant to do something. A ghost dance or sun dance or something like that. *Heya nico-wei, heya nico-wei, heya nico-wei hung-ee hei hei hei hei how.*

He hopped a little as he sang, arms raised up, but then went back to a slower stride. That felt more real, more ceremonial.

And then suddenly he was in the open, in the full moon, the dirt road white and luminous and the wide pool of water shining before him. The moon straight ahead, beckoning. He felt pulled toward it, felt acknowledged by the moon, recognized. The song had become a moon dance, and the moon had listened.

The moon was offering him a gift, this water. This was why he had been drawn here. The surface of the water always in motion, the light never still, but evolving in pattern. This is what Siddhartha had seen. In the passing of the water was the passing of self, of attachment, and in the shapes on the surface one could find the face of all things. Every longing, every pain, all of it would form for a moment, a trick of the light, and then dissolve. It was when we looked at water that we dreamed, and remembered the tug of previous incarnations, and what we longed for was our true form beyond this body, beyond this incarnation, beyond this world of illusions.

Galen understood now what he was meant to do tonight. The moonlight a path across the water, the proof, finally, of what he was. He walked toward it, or was walked toward it by the universe. The stream of beautiful sounds, the bubbling and coursing, a voice reassuring, the light soft, and he had lost his feet. They had become one with the light and would cross the surface in the same way that the light lay upon the water.

Galen ecstatic, his entire soul rushing with love. His foot at the surface, cold, the breath of the water, and that was all right, it was happening, but then his foot plunged through and he tilted, trying to keep his palms up, trying to save this, trying not to lose faith. The next step could hold, so he threw his other foot out there, but it plunged, also, and his ankle twisted on rock below and he was falling forward, hit the water face-first in an icy shock, all his air gone. He breathed water and pushed against rock and sand to get up, thrashing with his arms. He was coughing, stumbled and fell again, his ankle twisted and too difficult to stand on, so he propped on his butt and arms and pulled himself backward toward shore. He crawled out of the water and just lay in the dirt. What the fuck, he said. When is it going to happen?

Galen limped down the road, soaked and shivering and dirty, his wet jeans and sweatshirt heavy, and when he arrived at the cabin he wondered how he'd get in. He wasn't going in the front door. There was no way he was giving his aunt that satisfaction.

He wouldn't be able to take a bath, either. It was too late. So his only hope was the stove.

Galen stepped quietly onto the deck, ducked low under the main kitchen window and went around the side, peeked into the smaller window above the sink. He could see his mother and grandmother still sitting at the small yellow table, drinking yellow wine. A second bottle, almost empty. Everything distorted in the old glass of the window, bent, the upper part of a bottle magnified, lower part shrunken. His grandmother's head too small. Everything yellow, it seemed, even the white-painted walls cast yellow in the light.

It might be a while. They rarely drank, but when they did, it was back to the past. The cases of empty bottles from his grandfather, left outside the pantry door. Galen didn't have a single memory of him that was without wine, without that smell of Riesling, the only wine he'd drink, a piece of the old country. Galen didn't know where in Germany his grandfather was from, didn't know what it looked like, had no idea what his grandfather's childhood had been. All lost. An illusion anyway, but still, one Galen wanted to know, if only so that his grandfather could make more sense. His grandfather born into this world with a thick finger circling in the air, coming after Galen's belly, a buzzing sound, his grandfather saying *bzz*, *bzz*, *bzz*, and Galen terrified of that finger. The earliest memory, and of course flooded with the smell of that wine. His grandfather exhaling wine, his teeth dark, the thick hairs in his nostrils dark, trying to play, trying to show something like affection, but he was only terrifying, every part of him, his finger plunging far too hard into Galen's belly, a roughness to everything he did. Galen didn't have a single memory of his grandfather that didn't include fear.

Galen had only one memory, though, of actual violence. His grandfather pulling his grandmother around by her hair on the kitchen floor. Galen had laughed at first, when he ran into the kitchen and found them. It looked like a kind of game, something done for fun, except that the sounds didn't match that. His mother whisked him away quickly, out of the house, and every other memory that might have been of violence was only of sound and leaving.

Helen was right that men were the problem. Galen's grandfather the source of everything wrong in this family. But she couldn't say Galen was the same. That wasn't fair.

Galen was becoming far too caught up in the illusions. He needed to remember that none of this was real. His grandfather was only a touchstone, a marker, like the old stove or the big rock. Despair, getting depressed about his family, was only a kind of procrastination on the road. It was a refusal to keep moving, a distraction, a lack of courage to face lessons. It could feel real, but it wasn't real. You could spend an entire life trapped there, as his aunt had done, but that was an easy mistake, a weakness, a waste of an incarnation.

The wall behind the stove had a bit of warmth, even on the outside, so Galen stood flat against it, his cheek on the wood. His wet clothing so heavy and thick his body could warm the inside layer, perhaps, like a wetsuit. He was shaking, though. He just didn't have any reserves. No fat. He was not good with cold. He was meant to get in and quickly out of this incarnation. Just learn his final lessons and go. His body was not meant to last. Eating and pissing and shitting just a distraction, one he was tired of, his old soul frustrated at having to play the game again.

Galen hugged the cabin wall, tried to imagine his arms wrapping all the way around the entire structure. He waited and waited, desperately cold, and finally the light switched off, the window went dark. His lower jaw like a sewing machine. He waited another few minutes and then walked around back, let himself carefully in the door.

The kitchen air warmer but not as hot as he had hoped, the fire in the stove long since died. He sloughed off his wet clothing into the corner behind the door, then felt his way along the table in the dark, over to the drawers under the sink. Found the matches, lit one and set it on the stove for a light. He would start a new fire. He lifted one of the round burners with the chrome handle, and then the match went out and he was in darkness again. But he could feel hot air from the opening in the stove, and he set the burner carefully to the side, then felt with his hands. The cast iron warm on the surface, hotter still inside, so he bent over, the open hole of hot air at his chest, and hugged the stove. This would be enough. He wouldn't need a new fire. He felt the breath of the stove warm his chest and his belly, pressed his arms against its dry warm skin

until he had stopped shivering and creaked up the stairs to his bed
and slid under a pile of blankets. He loved the weight of the blankets, four layers thick, something he had only here at the cabin. He
curled into a fetal position, his head ducked under the covers, and
felt safe in his nest.

G alen awoke to the smell of bacon. Deep and beautiful smell, and he felt his hunger, the hollowness inside him. Bacon. There would be pancakes, also, and scrambled eggs. When he smelled the toast, it would be time. His mother trilling in the kitchen, her happy voice. Chatting with his grandmother, and he heard his aunt's voice, even. A time of peace. A new day.

Galen snuggled in the warmth of his blankets, even though the air had warmed from the stove. He waited until he could smell toast, and then he pulled the blankets aside and reached in his duffel for shorts and a shirt. He had no other pants, unfortunately. Only the jeans that were wet.

Galen, his mother called. She sang it, rising up on the first syllable, falling on the last. Ga-len. A happy time. And he felt willing to go along with it. He came down the stairs and found them all at the table, squeezed into his place and watched his plate fill with two pancakes, eggs, strips of bacon, and toast. A mug of hot chocolate.

Wow, he said.

Brekkie is served, his mother said. Brekkie the way the Schumachers do it.

Galen leaned over his plate and smelled his bacon, deep inhales and closed his eyes. His first meal in what felt like ages. He ate with his bare hands, didn't want to distance himself with a fork. Kept his face down close, nuzzled the hot pancakes and warm sticky syrup. Tasted the bacon, the smoke and salt and fat and meat, unbelievably good. He was humming, his insides coming alive.

The eggs moist, not overcooked, black pepper and garlic and onion. He twirled his tongue in his pile of eggs and then sucked them up, pushed the toast into his mouth. The combinations. Toast and eggs. Bacon and maple syrup.

Looks like my little pumpkin is enjoying his breakfast, his mother said.

Mm, he said. I love this. Thanks, Mom.

You need a good breakfast, his grandmother said. You're going off to school soon. He opened his eyes and looked up at her. She seemed so proud, smiling at him, her eyes glistening.

Yes, he said.

What are your classes?

I'm taking French poetry, he said. Because my year abroad will be in France, in Paris.

Ooh la la, his grandmother said, and elbowed his mother approvingly. She looked happier than she had in years. That sounds wonderful. And you deserve it. You've worked so hard.

Thank you, Grandma.

Where will you stay?

Galen had a bite of bacon, the smoky, fatty goodness in his mouth while he imagined where he would stay. The Sorbonne, he said.

Ooh, his grandmother said.

They're a sister university with my school. And the dorms are all on the top floor, built into those enormous roofs you see in Paris. The windows have wooden shutters from hundreds of years ago, and when you wake up, you can push those shutters open and look out over all of Paris.

I'm so happy for you. My handsome young man. Think of all the people you'll meet.

The year abroad is a ways off, his mother said.

But there's no harm in planning now, his aunt said. It really is grand. And you never know what could happen. Galen could become a professor at the Sorbonne if he likes Paris enough. I'm sure they would want him to stay.

Yes, of course, his grandmother said.

Well, his mother said. We have such a beautiful day today, with the sun out. After brekkie, shall we take a walk at Camp Sacramento?

I'd like to hear more about Paris, Jennifer said.

Me too, Helen said.

The year abroad includes a tutorial with a French poet. I have to have my French up to that level by then, so I'll be working hard over the next two years. Language study is something you have to work on every day.

Well, that will be no problem for you, his aunt said.

Galen took a large bite of pancake and thought he really could do this. He really could study French for two years and then spend a year in Paris and study with a poet. Only his mother was holding him back.

I actually need to send in a check next week, he said. Do you happen to have your checkbook, Grandma?

Oh, his grandmother said, looking startled. Oh yes, I'm sure I have that somewhere. Suzie-Q, where is my checkbook?

Galen's mother looked punched.

Next week is when Jennifer's payment for school is due also, Helen said. What a coincidence. You can write both checks at the same time.

Yes, Galen's grandmother said. Yes, of course. She looked worried. She knew something wasn't right, and Galen felt terrible for her now. This had gone out of control.

I think we left the checkbook at home, Mom, Galen's mother said. We'll have to do that when we get back.

I'm pretty sure you brought it, Helen said. I'll get your purse and be right back. She got up fast.

Helen, Galen's mother said, but Helen was gone toward her mother's bedroom. Galen's mother got up and went after her.

Galen's grandmother raised her eyebrows. Oh my, she said. I'm not sure what's happening.

It's okay, Grandma, Jennifer said. You're just writing checks for school, for Galen and me. Fall semester of college is about to start.

Oh. She looked at Jennifer, and Galen realized this was rare that she even looked at Jennifer. You're in college now? Are you that old?

I'm starting next month, Jennifer said.

You look so young. Where are you going to school?

Stanford.

Stanford. Oh my. How did you get into Stanford? You're not smart enough to get into Stanford, are you?

I did my homework. You helped me. We spent a lot of hours working together, Grandma. Jennifer reached out and held her grandmother's hand. Thank you so much for helping me, Grandma.

Oh. And where is Galen going?

Chico State.

Chico State?

Yeah. He doesn't like doing homework.

Stop it, Galen said. I'll be right back. He could hear his mother and aunt fighting in the back room, and he knew he needed to help his mother now.

He was almost at the hide-a-bed when they came crashing out

of his grandmother's bedroom. They both had their hands on a tan purse, large and sturdy and old, with big handles. His mother yanked hard, swinging his aunt. He'd never seen his mother like this, her mouth snarling, a strange combination with her happy flowered apron.

Then his aunt yanked and his mother hit the wall, slipped, and went down hard in the narrow gap between wall and bed, arms flailing. His aunt on the hide-a-bed now, and Galen charged, had one foot up on the mattress when she straight-armed and just ran right over him. Her face grim and determined, and he was falling, tilted too far backward, and his head hit and bounced, his skull too heavy, like a bowling ball, and he couldn't breathe or see. His head revving up inside, a high whine like a jet engine, and he was panicking. Had he heard a crack? Had he cracked his skull?

He didn't want to move.

Just playing, just having fun, he could hear his aunt saying. Just having a wrestle on the hide-a-bed, like when we were kids. Wonderful fun.

Suzie-Q? his grandmother called.

Galen needed to do something. His mother wasn't doing anything. Maybe she was hurt too. But his head was so heavy and pulsing. He could hear Jennifer saying something about Stanford, about the cost of Stanford. They were working her together.

Galen could feel his toes, was able to move his feet. And his hands. He wasn't paralyzed. His breath came back, and he opened his eyes and was still awake and could think. He was afraid to feel his head, afraid he'd find blood or even a crushed bit of skull, but he reached up and felt only a bump, swelling already, but no wetness. Dry hair. He would be okay, maybe.

Mom? he called.

Yeah, she said.

Why aren't you doing anything?

I hit my tailbone, she said. It hurts. But I also just can't fight anymore. They'll take some money, and maybe that's okay. If they try for more than fifty, it won't clear. I can't fight them anymore. I can't fight you anymore, either.

There's enough money to take fifty thousand and it wouldn't matter?

Stop.

I can't believe this. Why didn't I go to college?

You could have gotten a job. You could have gone. But you wanted to be taken care of.

Just like you.

Fine. I don't care what you think of me. Think anything you want.

You don't make any sense. How could I think anything about you? You're in crazyland. We have all this money available, and we aren't using it. Why are we living off the housekeeping and gardening checks?

No response from his mother.

Tell me, you piece of shit, Galen said in a low growl that only his mother would hear. You don't get to just not say anything. This is my life. My future. He had a desire to shake her. He wanted to shake her and rip her into pieces.

You won't talk to me that way.

I'll talk to you however I want until you stop acting like a crazy person.

The talking had stopped in the other room. They were having her sign, no doubt. He never should have mentioned the checkbook. But he had never thought of it before.

When we return home, his mother said, you're going to move out. You're going to find a job and a place to live. Or just sleep in the streets. I don't care.

Galen wanted to scream, but he kept his mouth closed. She wouldn't make him move out. He hated her power trips. He tried to just calm, stared at the ceiling, this crazy ceiling with the white-painted planks all going diagonal. It didn't make any sense. He'd never noticed it before. Another sign of crazy, but he'd never looked up and noticed.

Helen and Jennifer marched past out the front door. He heard the car doors slam and the engine rev up and they drove away.

Well, he said. I think I've had enough family time for today. He rose carefully, his head a big ball of throb.

Help me up, his mother said.

Help yourself up, he said, and went out the front door. Smell of dust in the air, so they must have taken off fast. He walked around the cabin on the blind side, away from the kitchen, and up into the trees. The dirt loose, his feet sinking. Something had mounded all the dirt everywhere, ants or moles or whatever else, and it was more sand than dirt, bits of granite forming a kind of dirt-froth. Nothing solid anywhere. He stepped over rotted trunks and limbs crumbling away in what looked almost like coals, a deep orange. Insects everywhere, the place infested.

He found a stand of smaller pines providing enough cover, braced against the largest of them, leaned over, pushed his finger back hard into his throat, and let all the piggy grease and egg drool and pancake and syrup come out, purged himself, made himself clean again. If only there were some way he could throw up his family and not have them inside him anymore.

he chicken and dumplings. His mother and grandmother began cooking, putting the world back together again. How many times? he wondered. How many times had they put the world back together? And why? Why not let it fall apart and stay apart, why not let the truth happen? It would be easier. They could all relax. Everyone could just say they hated each other and be done with it. But somehow that was not possible, and so his mother and grandmother chopped up two chickens at the sink.

Galen went down occasionally to watch, peeking around the corner from the stairs, and neither of them acknowledged his presence. He'd become a kind of ghost.

His mother chopping yellow onions at the sink, his grandmother sitting at the table peeling yellow potatoes. They were drinking wine again, a study in yellow again, even some of their clothing yellow. His grandmother's sweater, the edges of his mother's apron.

The crunch of the knife through onion, the slap of the peeler on a potato. No other sounds, and this was part of what made the world unbearable, the magnification of small sounds in a vacuum. This was one of the signs. Only a world that had been staged could be so flimsy and so annoying.

They were the same person, maybe, his mother and grandmother, a split image he needed to resolve and bring into focus. They had been created at the same time, in Galen's first memories when he was three or four, and they had a similar role. They had drifted further apart in recent years as his grandmother lost her mind. She had been left marooned on some positive sense of him, whereas his relationship with his mother had grown steadily worse. Were they the same, though, underneath all that?

If you're not doing anything, you can go chop some wood, his mother said. She was standing at the sink chopping carrots now, and didn't turn to look at him. He wasn't sure how she even knew he was here.

Okay, Galen said. His head hurt, but he liked the idea of getting away from the kitchen and his mother, and he liked chopping wood.

He went out the front door, walked around the deck to the toolshed. About the size of an outhouse, and older, even, than the cabin. No light inside, and he had to let his eyes adjust. Shovels, picks, several axes, as if this were a mining camp. All the tools old, the wood handles dark and polished from use. The fishing gear was in here, too, old wicker baskets and ancient poles. He didn't know how to use any of it. In all the times they'd come to the cabin while his grandfather was still alive, his grandfather had stayed in Carmichael and worked. Never retired. Had a stroke, finally, went to the rest home, and died. He'd been a civil engineer, designing highways and even that bridge in Sacramento that his grandmother was always mentioning, but what did that mean?

Galen pulled out the smallest axe and grabbed a wedge from the floor. Cold heavy steel, the edges of it dented and smashed from years of blows. Then he pushed the door shut with his foot and went to the chopping block behind the cabin. He dropped the wedge in the dirt and swung the axe over his head into the block.

He loved the feel of that swing, of the weight on the outer arc, his right hand slipping down on the smooth handle.

Yeah, he said.

The wood was stacked along the back wall of the cabin, with an overhang from the roof to keep it dry. Gray-looking because it'd been here so many years. Their visits were never very long. Galen grabbed a log and worried about spiders. He didn't have any gloves. He upended the wood on the chopping block and took a large swing with the axe. The blade glanced off the edge of the log and buried into the ground a few inches from his left foot.

Whoa, Galen said. He stepped back, the handle standing up, and looked behind him, as if someone might have seen. He had this dizzy feeling like tottering at the edge of a cliff, the air pulling him downward. Holy crap, he said. He looked at his old Converse sneakers, dirty canvas, so thin, and just couldn't believe how close he'd come to losing his foot. He had this awful feeling he could still lose it. He shook his arms, shaking off the heebie-jeebies, then picked up the axe again.

Anything could happen at any time. That was the truth of the world. You could just lose your foot one day, and after that you'd be a guy missing a foot. You could never know what was coming next, and that was true for even the smallest things. You couldn't know what thought you'd have next, or what someone would say in conversation, or what you might feel an hour from now, and this effect was always amplified by his mother. His conversations with her could go from zero to crazy in a few seconds. He didn't know why that was true only with her. She could be calling him pumpkin one minute and threatening to throw him out on the street the next. And when he felt angry at her, it came from some terrible source, something you'd never know about, never suspect, and then suddenly he was drowning in it.

Galen wanted peace with his mother. He wanted peace. But as soon as he came near her, he wanted to kill her.

He was more careful to keep his feet wide, stood farther away and focused on the top of the log as he swung. A satisfying *chock* this time as the blade hit. He used the wedge in the gap and swung again, split the wood in one stroke. Brighter flesh inside, the wood yellow instead of gray.

Okay, he said. And he worked into a rhythm, log after log, focusing carefully on the target, enjoying that swing, the high weightlessness of it, the feel of the muscles in his arms and back, the sweat on his skin, the sound of the blows muffled in the trees.

Earthly labor. That was perhaps the fastest path, because you could forget yourself, forget everyone, and feel only the swing. The key to getting through the world was to find a way to forget that it existed. A shadow in a shadowland, biding time.

Galen flung the axe up the hill. Just an impulse. End over end through the air, *whump*ing into the earth. He hiked up to it and flung it again, the blade and handle flipping through branches and bouncing in the dirt, spraying small grains of granite. Puffs of dust like smoke. The axe-flinger. He didn't know what it meant, but it felt good. It felt right. He threw the axe as hard as he could, hurled it with both hands. He was like Thor, splitting the air itself. Tearing through appearances, ripping the fabric of the illusion.

Galen glanced quickly behind to see the wake left in the air, any swirl or disturbance at the edges of where he had passed, but his eyes were not trained to see. Troughs and rips and back eddies, and all of it hidden from the naked eye. But the axe might cut through quickly enough. If he focused just behind it as it flew, he might see something.

He threw again and everything was just too fast. Even the flipping of the handle rotating beyond the speed at which he could isolate an image. He needed to learn how to slow the world down in order to see it. His blood pounding now from running after the axe. The dust in his nostrils. His feet sinking in the tufted earth, bogging him down.

If he could throw and get the blade to stick into a tree, the sudden halting might reveal something. He might catch the eddy just behind the shaft as it washed over. The abruptness might allow vision.

So Galen held the axe behind him, hefted it a bit in the air to gauge its weight, its balance, stepped forward and flung at a trunk twenty feet away. But the axe went wide and bounced end over end in the dirt.

Galen walked instead of ran, getting tired. But he could hear the wind rising in the pines all around him, clouds moving over and the day become darker suddenly, and he felt he was at the edge of something. A tree farther ahead had lower dead branches covered in a bright lime green moss. Glowing arms in the overcast, muted light. They were emanating, luminous. They looked unreal.

Galen stood with the axe before this tree and tried to know the trunk, tried to lock it into place in the air and feel its pull, and when he flung, he felt the flipping end over end until the axe hit, handle first, glanced off into dirt and ferns.

Close, he said. I'm getting close here.

He retrieved the axe, walked back again to his position, and opened himself to a universe made almost entirely of empty space. Neutrons and protons, or whatever, swirling around, electrical and magnetic connections all that was holding us together, and no reason that couldn't be cleaved in an instant, revealed. He threw the axe with all his might, end over end through emptiness, slowing and seeing, and the blade connected with trunk, abruptly halted, the handle frozen in place, the eddy of air washed over the handle, the seam in what had been cleaved, but it was already memory, already gone. He just wasn't fast enough. He needed to be able to pause in a moment like that and travel around in it, float for a while, and that never happened. His axe hanging from the trunk, the bright green arms above, all of it a perfect moment, and all of it passed and gone, as if it had never been.

The mafia didn't return until late afternoon. Galen's mother and grandmother on a walk at Camp Sacramento, the stew pot in the oven, smell of chicken and onion in the air, and Galen settled upstairs with *Jonathan Livingston Seagull*.

Anyone here? his aunt called out.

Yeah, he said. I'm reading. The others are on a walk.

No response after that. They settled in below and he stayed above, and that was good.

Jonathan Livingston Seagull didn't like to fight over scraps with the other seagulls. They were all obsessed with food, but he was free of that. He was testing the limits of gravity and physics, experimenting in his flight, trying to get the world to slip, trying to catch the unreality of it, just like Galen. Jonathan had midair tumbles and frustrations, just like Galen's crashing into the water. The amazing thing was that Galen came first, not the book. He was already doing all of these things before he read the book. And so the book was a kind of recognition.

What amazed Galen most was that although the entire book was a kind of metaphor—it was about seagulls, after all—Galen was living it in real life. He was living in a time that was preparing to recognize him. That was an important part about being a prophet. It was no good if you had the vision and no one could understand it. But books like this one were preparing people to understand Galen.

Galen rested the book on his chest and listened. He had his earphones in, listening to a nature tape of waves at the seashore. He listened to this whenever he read *Jonathan Livingston Seagull*, and in the sound of the waves, he could hear the impermanence of things. The forming and crashing, remaking and dissolution of the world. The self put together in the same flimsy way. The key was to feel the ebb and tug as everything receded before it built again and lumbered forward. Because in that ebb, at the very end of it, at the end of the pull, was the nothingness that was truth. Samsara, suffering, was the inability to stay in that moment. Samsara was the forming of the next wave.

A hand on his crotch and he jolted upright, eyes open. Jennifer laughing. You looked so peaceful, she said. She took a step closer and yanked his headphones out of the tape recorder. Wave sounds in the bad speakers, sounding like static. That's really beautiful, she said.

Galen pushed stop and the play lever clicked up.

You're reading about seagulls, she said, and listening to waves. How is that being here now in the mountains?

Her hair was wet and she smelled like coconut. Her eyes bright and blue. She sat on the bed and he watched her breasts under her T-shirt.

I was meditating, he said.

Meditating on these, she said, and held her breasts. She crawled up over him, lifted her T-shirt, and put her breasts in his face.

Hot still from her bath, damp, but her nipples going hard in the cool air. She rocked back and forth, slapping his cheeks with her breasts, so soft, so unbelievably soft, and he grabbed a nipple in his mouth, wasn't sure what to do, but he had his lips around it, careful not to use his teeth, and he sucked.

Mm, she said. A little weird, but it feels kind of good. I like the whiskers, too. Try just licking.

So he licked.

That's kind of nice, too. Circle my nipple with your tongue. And she grabbed a breast and held it in his mouth.

Mm, she said.

He liked the little bumps around her nipple, but he pulled his face away. Quiet, he whispered. Your mom might hear.

She's on a hike. We have the place to ourselves.

Wow.

Yeah, maybe you'll get lucky this time.

I hope, Galen said. I hope. And he had a breast back in his mouth.

Hold on a sec, she said, and got off the bed, went downstairs.

What happened?

She reemerged holding a cassette tape. The Cars, she said. I like to listen to the Cars when I have sex.

When you have sex, he said.

Your lucky day. Your last day as a virgin. You happen to be the only cock available, and I feel good. I'm rich now. We just deposited two hundred thousand dollars.

Two hundred thousand?

Yep.

Holy fuck.

We're getting a house, and I'm going to college. And we don't have to put up with your mom's shit ever again. And Grandma can fucking die, the old bitch. She'll never see us again. You won't see us again either. So this is your one lucky day. The best pussy you'll ever get. Even the Buddha would fuck this.

Galen just nodded. He didn't want to say anything to wreck it.

And he knew they'd still see plenty of Helen and Jennifer once the check bounced. They'd been too greedy.

Jennifer put the Cars in and hit play. It was on "Drive" from *Heartbeat City*, and even with the crap speakers the music filled the place, turned the air into something else, a different mood. "Who's gonna drive you home . . . tonight." Get off the bed, she said, so he did. She dropped her sweatpants and panties, kept her shirt lifted above her breasts, and lay back across the bed.

Kneel on the floor and lick me, she said. And then you can fuck me, but you can't lie down on me. You're too disgusting. You can only touch me with your cock and your tongue. That's it. I can't even look at you. She closed her eyes.

Thank you, Galen said, getting down on his knees.

This was as close as he would ever come to a shrine, he realized. This was the sacred, right here, her legs spread. He pushed her legs up, had her spread as far as she would go, the pink exposed, and just ran his lips and tongue over everything, the most beautiful moment of his life. The Cars crooning, her hot wet flesh in his mouth, and all he'd read about in *Hustler* and *Playboy* and *Penthouse* was coming true. Her clit really was there, nubby and eager, like a mini boner, and he could get her to jerk and curl when he sucked at it, and her asshole puckered more tightly when he licked.

Fuck me, she said, the most beautiful words ever uttered, and he dropped his underwear and pushed her legs back hard and spread and pushed his dick in and just couldn't believe how silky she was, how perfect and hot and soft. He was all the way in and just stayed there.

Keep fucking, she said.

I have to feel this, he said. I just need a moment.

Don't be a pussy, she said. And don't come. Just start fucking me. There was something about the geometry of this, pushing her legs back at forty-five-degree angles, how she was exposed and flat, facing the ceiling, and he was coming in at this angle. Something about watching was as good as feeling.

Fuck me, damn it.

He pulled out slowly, feeling the soft slide, and she was tight around him, gripping him, and then he pushed back in, pushed in as deep as he could, felt his tip bump into the back wall.

Aah, she said. Yeah. He pulled out again, all the way out, and it felt good to enter again, so he just did that, just the tip, an inch or so in, and kept pulling out.

Yeah, she said.

I can't feel my feet anymore, he said. I can hardly feel my legs.

Shut up, she said.

Then he plunged all the way in again, ground his hips against hers, rocked around in a circle. My crown chakra is totally open. Oh my god. I can feel this all along my spine.

Shut up. I'm serious. I hate the sound of your voice.

So he tried to shut up, but he just couldn't. I feel so aligned, he said. He pushed in harder, started moving faster, and he could feel himself tightening throughout his body, golden strings from every limb, from the top of his head and all along his spine, being pulled into his balls.

I'm fucking you, he said. I'm fucking you hard now.

Uh, uh, uh, she was saying.

He looked over and saw his mother on the stairs. Watching him.

He stopped moving, and this made everything gather and his dick started pulsing and he knew he was going to come. He couldn't stop it now. He pulled out and came in jerks onto Jennifer while he looked at his mother. He couldn't stop his mouth from opening in a fuck-grimace, couldn't hold back the moaning. His mother seeing his face like this.

Uh, Jennifer said. I'm not done, damn it. Get down on your knees and lick. I'm not done yet.

Galen's mother stepped back down the stairs, her sound covered by the Cars, and he got on his knees and licked. His come all over her belly, the smell of it, and he was still twitching. Jennifer grabbing his head and humping it. Difficult to keep his tongue in the right place, but he did his best. She wrapped her thighs around his head, mashing his ears, and he couldn't hear a thing. Just struggling to keep his tongue out there and finally she bucked and yanked at his head as she came.

He pushed her thighs apart and managed to free his head. She had her eyes closed, head curled to her shoulder, her hands on her crotch. Her breasts so perfect and beautiful, all the soft lines of her, and he felt very sad, because he knew he'd never get to do this again. His mother would stop it from happening. He didn't know what she'd do, but she'd do something. She would certainly do something. So he took a last look, ran his hands along the soft skin of Jennifer's thighs.

Aah, Jennifer was saying. Aah. She was stroking herself with both hands, prolonging it, and she wasn't being all that quiet. Galen wondered whether his grandmother could hear these sounds over the music.

He stood there and looked down at his dick, hard still. He wanted to put it in, wanted to feel her again, so he did that.

Yeah, she said. Yeah.

Silky was the only word for it. He moved slowly, feeling every moment, and he put his hands on her breasts, last time he'd have them in his hands, and he felt so sad. She was mean to him, but he loved her. Loved her unconsciousness, her roughness in the world, loved her selfishness. And she was out of his league, of course. If she weren't his cousin, he'd never have had a chance. She was the luckiest he would ever get.

He lay down on her, and she let him. She wrapped her arms around his back, and that felt unbelievably good. He felt loved. He kissed her neck and held her hips in his hands while he pushed in as far as he could, and he could feel her building again, a panting in her breath and tightening all along her back and thighs, clinging to him. He wanted it never to end, wanted her always to cling to him like this, but then she came, tightening around him, pulsing, jerking, and moaning from deep in her throat.

Oh, she said. Oh. And then she was pushing up at his chest, pushing him off. I can't breathe, she said. Get off me.

So he pulled out and rolled to the side on the bed, his feet on the floor. The end. He closed his eyes and tried to record everything, tried not to forget or lose a single moment. He wanted to relive this, even now. He wanted to preserve all of it.

Shh, Jennifer said and sat up abruptly. I think I hear something, she whispered. Someone might be back. She grabbed the roll of toilet paper off his nightstand and wiped away his come. Disgusting, she said.

She yanked down her shirt, pulled on her panties and sweatpants in a flash, and then asked him if there was anything on her face.

No, he said, and he lay back down and she left.

Samsara. And yet Galen knew he would spend every day like this, for the rest of his life, if he could. He would choose it above transcendence. Transcendence was only a consolation prize for those who couldn't find good enough samsara.

The Cars were still crooning, but it was too sad now. He couldn't bear it. So he clicked the tape recorder off, and now he could hear dishes in the kitchen.

He lay on his bed, thinking perhaps this was the prophet he was meant to be, the prophet who would free everyone from religion and send them back to bed for more sex. The prophet who would expose the sham of transcendence. But he knew this was only the boner thinking. It was still there, with no signs of fading. A sad reminder of what Galen had just had and would never have again.

What surprised him most was that he really did love her. She was the most unlikable person, but he loved her anyway. He didn't understand how that had happened. His first love, no longer a virgin. But why couldn't he have fallen in love with someone who wasn't his cousin, or someone who was nice to him? And what was it about sex that increased his love for her? He felt so vulnerable now, his chakras all wide open, exposed. The thought that he would never be with her like that again felt so heavy he began to cry. He buried his face in his pillow and sobbed as quietly as he could, and he felt how unfair the world is to those who truly love.

The chicken and dumplings. Finally arrived. The stew pot on the stove, lid open, and Galen loved the fluffy white dumplings floating on the surface like clouds. Pure and white, browned along their edges and peaks. He lifted one carefully with the serving spoon onto his plate. The underside slick with gravy. The entire stew a thick gravy with chicken and potatoes, carrots and onions, and he heaped his plate. This is what he would have instead of Jennifer. Food.

He couldn't look at Jennifer, couldn't look at his mother. All of them crammed at that small yellow table, and he kept his eyes on his food.

You've done yourself proud, Mom, Galen's mother said. But there was no real cheer in her voice.

I don't know, his grandmother said. Something doesn't seem quite right. But I can't remember, of course, what it should be. I can't remember anything. Sometimes I wish I could just die. I hate not remembering anything.

Mom, Galen's mother said. Don't say that.

Yeah, Grandma, Galen said. It tastes great. It's just like before. And this was true. He was savoring the rich gravy and chicken, the onions and potatoes turned almost to mush after stewing all day.

I have this awful feeling about something, but I don't even know what it's about.

Everything's fine, Mom.

It's like I can't remember what I have to fear. Like some mouse wandering around forgetting there's a cat but feeling afraid of the cat anyway.

That would be Suzie-Q, Helen said. Suzie-Q is the cat.

Don't start, Galen's mother said.

Suzie-Q is taking you back to the rest home after this. Your health is fine, and you could live at home, but Suzie-Q doesn't want you at home. She wants you in the rest home so she can take your money.

Galen's mother slumped and looked down at her food.

Is that true?

No, Mom, it's not true. Helen hates me, and she hates you, so she tells lies.

Helen doesn't hate me. She's my daughter. Why are you saying ugly things like that?

Galen's mother put both hands over her face, elbows on the table, blocking out the world. Mom, I can't do this, she said. Helen is the enemy. I'm not the enemy.

Look at that, Mom, Helen said. Calling me the enemy. Who calls her own sister the enemy? Is that how family treat each other?

She's right, Suzie-Q. Apologize to your sister right now.

Galen's mother's face hidden in her hands, her back and chest caving between her shoulders.

You apologize right this instant, Suzie-Q!

Galen wanted to help his mother, but he didn't know how. His grandmother was angry now, and she thought she was on solid ground. She thought she knew what the problem was, and maybe that was better than not knowing.

She already said she was sorry, Galen said.

What?

She already said she was sorry, but you keep asking her to apologize, so now she's crying.

Oh, fuck me, Helen said. You can't switch it around that easily. Suzie-Q needs to apologize to me, Mom. She hasn't said she's sorry.

Watch your language, Helen.

Fuck you, Mom. If your memory really is this bad, then it won't matter what I say now. I can say something else tomorrow.

Helen!

Helen what? What are you going to do, Mom? You've already destroyed my life, and I've already taken your money now, so I don't need you anymore. You're the worst mother the world has ever seen. And do you know why that is?

Stop it, Helen, Galen's mother said. You won't treat her this way.

Focus, Mom. Do you know why it is that you're the worst mother ever?

How can you talk to me like this? Aren't you my daughter?

That's the thing. I am your daughter, and you didn't protect me. That's why you're the worst mother ever. Because I'm your daughter and you didn't do anything to protect me.

You're the worst grandmother, too, Jennifer piped in. You're in love with Galen because he has a dick, but you don't even know I'm here.

Galen's grandmother was shaking her head. Her eyes were wet. No, she said. No.

This is that cat you were afraid of, Mom, Helen said. The cat is the truth. The truth about you and who you are.

We all want you to die, Jennifer said in a voice that sounded loving and caring, which made it all the more frightening. She reached out and touched her grandmother's hand. We're all waiting for you to die.

Galen's grandmother jerked back as if bitten. She was on her feet, her chair fallen backward onto the floor. She was holding the hand that Jennifer had touched, holding it close against her, protectively. I have to get away from you, she said. I have to get away from all of you.

She opened the back door and ran out. She was fast.

Galen's mother rose to follow, but Helen grabbed her arm and yanked her down onto the floor. No you don't, she said. Galen's mother tried to crawl, but Helen dove onto her and flattened her. No Suzie-Q to the rescue, Helen said. That's never happening again.

Galen couldn't believe any of this was happening. It was like some ridiculous Big Time Wrestling match, and he was supposed to tag-team. He tried to get to his mother, but Jennifer punched him hard in the side of the head.

Fuck, he said. That hurts. He turned away, and she punched him in the back.

Stop it, he said, and he tried to get away from her. He was backing toward the front door, his hands out, trying to protect, but she was slapping them away. How could you do that? he asked. I love you.

Jennifer laughed. Right there in front of him, only an hour or two after they had made love. She laughed, and she was enjoying this, enjoyed hitting him.

I don't understand you, he said.

Oh, look at you, she said. How cute. She was talking to him as if he were a child or a small dog, her eyebrows way up and head tilted. This is how we show love in this family. Welcome to the family. Then she punched him in the neck.

Galen escaped out the front door and tried to breathe. He was staggering around trying to suck for air, and his throat felt crushed.

He collapsed against the railing and just held on, and then he got a breath. The air rushed in, painful. He wasn't going to die.

He needed to find his grandmother. She could be wandering around anywhere, and if she went too far, she'd forget which way she'd come. And it was cold.

Around the deck and past the shed, up through trees into the meadow. Moonlight a bright opaque white on every surface, the world turned into marble, become a solid. The cold air slipping. Grandma, he called, but his voice was weak, his throat damaged.

He humped across the meadow, bogged down in granite sand. Shadows everywhere, and the world could be seen two ways, the light or the shadows. Shapes born and landed, or the dark spaces around them, hollows that fell back infinitely. His grandmother could be either, and he didn't know how to look for her.

The hillside was tilting as he ran, his arms out for balance. He was exploding through solidity, his feet breaking apart the marble and scattering it. Somewhere in this maze she was doing the same, and he needed to sense her, catch a glimpse of the spray she kicked up in the light. Wave patterns, and somewhere she was carving the pattern, setting up a counterwave, and that was what he needed to feel. He needed to extend himself into the pattern and feel the dimpling at an edge. Grandma!

Mired in place, pinned down by gravity. Too slow, too limited by breath, too limited by this clunky body, by chicken fat and dumplings. Galen stopped and bent over, purged, tried to free himself, tried to lose this mortal shell. The air cold enough she'd never survive the night.

Too difficult to run uphill, so he turned to the side, traversed. Light and shadow, the world veering in and out of focus. He stopped and tried to squint into the high contrast and turn slowly in a circle and just look for movement. But the forest was motionless, as if the planet itself had stopped rotating. A slow drift through space, so quiet, the only sounds his own blood and breath, the tilting coming from inside him. The forest had swallowed her in stillness.

Grandma, he called again, and he began to feel angry. He shouldn't have to find her. He ran as fast as he could, running blindly now, no longer trying to see, crashing through branches and snags. She was out here somewhere, but with each moment, she became less likely.

He tried to listen, bent over and panting, and then he ran back the way he had come.

Farther than he had thought. Time wasted, and nothing looked familiar. He would spend all night searching, he knew, and he would never find her. She would be lost and gone.

But then he saw the big rock, staggered through the meadow, and realized where she must have gone. A path at the top of the meadow that led to other cabins and a trailhead. There was no other option, really. He'd been wasting his time, stupidly, and she'd be getting frightened by now. If she became frightened enough, she might leave the trail.

He followed this trail uphill, moving as fast as he could, passed cabins empty, boarded up, storm shutters all around, no glass to reflect the moon, only dull wood glowing white. He could smell this place, smell the dirt and weeds and pines, the familiar air and familiar path, and ahead, nearing the trail that went higher to the summit, he saw a figure passing from light to shadow to light.

Grandma, he called, and the figure paused, half in the light, herself become a half-moon. Grandma, he called again, wait for me.

She began moving again, and he ran after, tried not to lose sight of her. She could fade away so easily, a trick of the light. Wait for me, he called. And she disappeared, stopped in a shadow perhaps.

His lungs and throat ragged, no breath left at all, but he went as fast as he could toward where he had last seen her. The forest stretching, the space becoming farther. He thought he saw movement again, a dappling, but couldn't know for sure because of his own movement.

Grandma! he called. Wait for me! But he'd lost her, vanished into the shadows. He was coming close to where he'd seen her, and there was nothing. Whatever he'd seen, he'd only imagined it.

The trailhead began here, a narrower path up through forest and then exposed ridgelines of granite. The trail went for miles, and she could be anywhere along it. Or she might have gone the other direction, down to the creek, and followed that, or could be walking along the highway, even.

Galen didn't feel powerful at all, didn't feel he could extend into this forest. He was limited to one tiny point. But he was committed now to this path, and he hoped she would be on it.

A path of memory, a trail he'd followed hundreds of times from when he first began. The tree at the first bend, the open section with low growth on either side, the boggy ford across a small creek, the cabbagey plants growing out of thick mud, wide curls and folds to their leaves. The short section of meadow, the trail turning uphill again and now the granite steps, loose rocks but these low shelves, wound with roots. The scraping of his shoes, grinding the same steps from his earliest memories, but never before in moonlight. A familiar place become foreign.

Galen climbed the granite, the twists and turns in a narrow chute with growth in close on both sides, and nearly stepped on his grandmother.

Aah! he yelled. Holy shit. You scared me.

Galen, she said. With her light sweater and slacks, sitting on the trail, she looked like a piece of granite, a small boulder.

Wow, he said.

I don't know if I want to walk much farther, she said. I'm getting tired, and I'm cold. Why are we hiking at night?

We can go back.

But your mother is up ahead. We can't just leave her. She won't know to turn around.

She's not up there.

Yes she is. She's the one who wanted to go on this hike.

Grandma. It's only me and you.

No. Your mother is just ahead of me.

Mom is back at the cabin.

But I was just following her. If she's not up there, then what am I doing? Where am I going?

We're just taking a hike, just me and you.

Galen's grandmother stood up and looked away to the side, past all the small growth in close and out to mountain ranges that seemed to float on their own against the sky. It's not a hike, is it, she said.

No.

I was lost.

Yes.

And I would have just kept going, thinking your mother was ahead of me.

Maybe.

And why did I come out here? Why did I leave in the middle of the night?

Because Mom and Helen were fighting. You wanted to get away, which was a good choice. I think you did the right thing.

Do you know what it's like to not remember?

No.

It's like being no one, but still having to live anyway.

Grandma.

It really is that bad. It's like being no one. You think you're some-one now, but it's only because you can put your memories together. You put them together and you think that makes something. But take away the memories, or even scramble them out of order, and there's nothing left.

You remembered this trail. And you remembered the cabin when we first arrived. You remembered how to turn on the water.

Did I? Galen could see her smile for a moment. I can remem-ber places, I think. I do remember this trail. And I can recognize people. I haven't forgotten who you are. I just can't remember any-thing that's happened.

Well you've been a wonderful grandmother. I have a thousand great memories of time with you.

Galen's grandmother put her hand up to her mouth and closed her eyes. Galen looked away and waited. The mountains floating independently. The air colder now.

A deep exhale from his grandmother, and another. Okay, she said. Let's go home.

n the morning, Galen's mother announced they were packing up and leaving.

But we're having so much fun, Helen said. I'm really enjoying the cabin. Couldn't we stay another day or two?

Why are we leaving? Galen's grandmother asked.

I'll pack the kitchen, Galen's mother said. Mom, you can help me.

I'd like more bacon, Jennifer said.

Breakfast is over.

No it's not. My daughter wants more bacon, so fix her more bacon, little Suzie-Q.

Breakfast is over.

Mom can do it then. Mom, fix your granddaughter more bacon.

Don't speak to me that way.

Let me tell you a little story, Mom. There was a cat. Do you remember the cat?

What are you talking about?

Mom, ignore her. Let's pack the cupboards. I'll go get the boxes from the trunk.

This cat was blind and deaf. Outrageous shit happened in cat-world all the time, but the cat didn't hear or see anything.

We're going home, Helen, and if you want a ride in my car, you'll stop right now.

Golly, sis, I'm only trying to talk about my feelings.

I've heard enough. I can't do this anymore. I'm leaving in ten minutes. Ten minutes. All this kitchen crap can stay. You each have ten minutes to get in the car with your stuff. Grab your purse, Mom, and Galen will help you with your bag.

Then she was gone up the stairs.

Well, Helen said. I guess we're leaving. It is her car, after all, and she has the keys. It's hard to change that.

I don't know what's happening.

Your daughter is trying to rescue you from me. But I'm your daughter, too. It's a funny thing, isn't it? And a tad unjust, given the past.

I don't understand.

Yeah, well, that's nice for you. I think you've intentionally forgotten everything. Because how can you be responsible if you can't remember?

Let's go, Grandma, Galen said. I'll help you pack your bag in your room.

It's the new Suzie-Q, to the rescue.

We have to go now, Grandma.

What I want, Helen said, since that's what everyone's interested in, what I want is for everything to be undone. That's the level of responsibility I'm looking for.

Galen took his grandmother's arm and she rose, finally. I'm sorry, Helen, she said. Whatever it is, I'm sorry, okay?

Don't give me that snotty attitude, Mom. I'll be satisfied when you can go back and make everything not have happened. That's when you'll have apologized to me.

Galen pulled his grandmother away into the front room and then the bedroom. He helped her pack her small bag with a few bits of clothing.

I don't feel well, she said.

What's wrong? he asked. Are you sick?

No. Not sick, I guess. But I don't feel right. I feel awful.

I'm sorry, Grandma. He zipped up the bag and handed her the tan purse. That's everything, he said. We'll go out to the car now. Follow me.

He was ready to fight Helen if he had to, but she hadn't come into the front room yet. He and his grandmother scooted along the space between hide-a-bed and wall and made it outside. He put her bag in the trunk and opened the front passenger door.

We're leaving now? she asked.

Yeah. Just a few minutes. I'll be right back.

Okay, she said, and sat down, and he closed the door and she waited there with her purse on her lap.

They were in the front room now, busy gathering their stuff, not paying him any attention. He made it up to his bedroom and his mother was at the top of the stairs, her suitcase in hand.

Sorry, he said, but she didn't respond. Just waited for him to step past, then went down the stairs. So he gathered his things into the duffel and then lay back on his bed for a moment. Kind of dizzying, all that had happened on a short trip. But the part he'd never forget was sex with Jennifer. The high point of his life. Her legs spread right here on this bed.

Galen had a boner now, and the timing didn't seem appropriate, but he went ahead and jacked off anyway, moving quickly, remembering how Jennifer had felt and looked. Preserving his memories, keeping the recording fresh. He wanted to remember this right into his old age. He wanted to be jacking off on his deathbed remembering Jennifer at seventeen.

He cleaned up with the toilet paper but then wasn't sure where to put it. The garbage had already been emptied, and no more fires in the stove. It would smell if he left it, and they'd be able to smell it in the car if he brought it with him.

He went down the staircase with his duffel in front in one hand and the wad of toilet paper held behind his back. At the base of the stairs, he looked both ways and no one was around. So he slipped through the kitchen and hopped out near the toolshed, where he threw the wad on the ground for the chipmunks. It might help insulate a chipmunk's den or nest or whatever they had. Then he turned off the water up at the pipe and walked down to the deck, where he ran into his mother.

I already turned off the water, he said.

She didn't say anything. She looked like she wasn't even his mother. No recognition, no one home. Just turned around, walked past the car to the spigot to let all the water run out, then got in the car and Galen pushed into the back with Helen and Jennifer and they were off.

Good-bye, cabin, Galen said, as they always did, but it didn't have the usual jolly feel.

They rumbled down the dirt road and across the bridge, Galen trying to catch glimpses of trout in the creek. My lance, he said. I forgot my lance.

No response from his mother.

We have to go back, he said, but she continued on, over the bridge, pulled onto the highway and the air rushed in. I still haven't caught a trout, he yelled over all the sound. Damn it.

They came around the bend with the view of Lover's Leap,

where a squaw had tumbled down granite in grief at losing her lover, but Galen was on the wrong side of the car and couldn't see much past the mafia. He stuck his head out the window like a dog, let his cheeks blow open in the warm air, and could see Horsetail Falls, just a quick glimpse. He had meant to hike up there this trip.

He pulled his head back in. I wanted to hike Horsetail, he yelled. Why are we leaving so early?

His family had turned into stone, though, no one capable of speech. Fine, he said.

They fell down through mountains into the lower foothills, gray pines a pale green, daubed into the forest as if they'd been watercolored. Nearing Sam's restaurant, which had every video game imaginable, including ones you couldn't find anywhere else. An antiaircraft one that used actual movies of planes. If you lined up correctly when you fired, the film would cut to footage of a fireball, the plane exploding. Can we stop at Sam's? he asked.

No response. No one had said anything the entire drive. All in their own thoughts, or not having any thoughts. Apparitions on pause. Jennifer's thigh against his, and he felt like he had already lost her, felt this restless despair that made him want to just start howling. But he tried to hold it together. He didn't know what was going to happen today, didn't know what his mother was going to do.

As they crested the final hill, they could look out over the Central Valley, endless flat expanse of dry yellow grass with irrigated patches. It was a desert. The furnace air blasting in the windows. A version of hell, and why had anyone settled here? Just because it was easier to plant on flat ground instead of a hill? He didn't understand. The entire valley a self-selected internment camp for the stupid and the poor. But his grandparents had money and education and ended up here. Perhaps because they were both immigrants and didn't know better. What Galen didn't understand was why he had manifested this place and this history. What could possibly be learned from it? Why put himself here? Why make himself suffer?

Home sweet home, he yelled over the wind.

No response, of course.

Home on the prairie, he yelled. Home on Mars. Hell-home.

Apparently nothing he said could provoke any response.

I'm a midget, he yelled. I'm a bunny. I'm a coelacanth.

You're a small turd, his aunt yelled.

Finally, he yelled back. A bit of conversation. Thank you.

An entitled turd, his aunt continued. A small, entitled turd. A dried, entitled turd. Hey, it rhymes. We're all poets.

Galen wondered what it would be like to strangle someone, to have a throat in his hands and just keep pressing in with his thumbs. It was difficult, probably. More rigid than you'd expect, not easy to crush the windpipe. But he'd be willing to give it his all.

He looked over at his aunt, but she was looking out her side window. Jennifer was smiling, laughing at him probably. Real nice that that would be their last moment together.

So he stared out his own window at uninspired suburbs until they were passing Bel-Air.

They have the best pumpkin pies, he said.

Yes, his grandmother said, yes they do. They have the most wonderful pies. And I think we're out of pie. We should stop.

Galen's mother kept driving.

Suzie-Q, we need to stop at Bel-Air.

We just drove all the way from the cabin, Mom. We need to get you settled in and get home and unpack.

It's been so long since I've tasted pumpkin pie, Galen said.

Yes, his grandmother said. It's been too long. Turn around right now, Suzie-Q.

Galen's mother looked at him in the rearview, a bereaved look, not what he was expecting. Your chicken and dumplings were wonderful, Mom, she finally said.

What?

We had such a nice visit at the cabin, and I just loved your chicken and dumplings. The dumplings were perfect.

Well, his grandmother said. Well, that's nice.

Bel-Air was long gone, and soon enough they were at the rest home, concrete block of despair, a place to give up and be forgotten. Galen had in fact forgotten they were returning here. He was getting used to having his grandmother around.

Why are we bringing her here? he asked.

What is this place? his grandmother asked. I know this place. Is this a hospital?

Galen's mother didn't answer, just pulled up in front and got out. She grabbed her mother's bag from the trunk, then opened her mother's door.

What are we doing? Galen's grandmother asked.

We're home.

This isn't home.

This is home.

I don't like this place. You take me home right now, Suzie-Q.

This is home, Mom.

Why are you doing this to me?

Galen couldn't bear to listen. She was pleading now. Let's take her home, he said.

But his mother simply ignored him. She took her mother carefully by the arm. Come on, Mom, she said, and helped her out of the car. There. We'll get you all settled in.

Galen's grandmother looked back at him. I don't like this place, she said.

Why are we putting her here? Galen demanded.

Because she walked into the forest at night and would have kept going and died. Because she could do that at home, too. I found my mother this nice place because I love her and I want her to be safe. I don't want her to be hurt.

Galen believed her for once. Her mouth open and ragged, tired, and he could see how worried she'd been last night. He hadn't realized that before. She'd been afraid she'd lose her mother. Galen felt uncomfortable. He had a sense of his mother's goodness, and he didn't like to think of his mother's goodness.

His mother and grandmother walked away into that awful place. Prison and hospital combined. A place of a thousand voices, none of them talking to each other. His grandmother curtained away in her white linoleum semicircle, waiting. Looking ahead to ten or twenty years of waiting.

She shouldn't be here, Galen said. It's better to maybe wander off and die than just wait here in a prison.

That's true, Helen said. She's still my mother.

She's a bitch, Jennifer said. Who cares what happens to her.

Yeah, Helen said. Maybe you're right.

What if Jennifer says that about you someday?

Huh, Helen said.

I wouldn't do that, Mom.

You might. It's true. You might. And that's fine.

The engine was cooling off, pinging, and it seemed that all its heat was being transferred to the interior of the car. Galen's entire body was a slick. The windows down, but no breeze, and the outside air almost as hot.

Galen opened his door and stepped out, dizzy. Jennifer followed, her face wet with sweat, hair up in a ponytail. We're getting a place with air-conditioning, she said. I don't care where the house is, or how big it is, but it has to have air-conditioning.

Galen walked in a slow circle in the sun. There was no shade. The black pavement radiating. Humans had invented all the shittiest ways to live. Rest homes, cars, pavement, stuck in deserts like this, places you wouldn't want to live even one more day. It would have been a better plan to walk around naked and never invent anything. That way, you'd have to head for a creek or a lake or at least some trees. You'd never just stand around in a thousand-mile oven.

I can't believe she's here, Galen said. And I can't believe this fucking pavement.

Whoa, Jennifer said.

I'm serious. Every square foot is nothing less than tragic. It's a sign of how fundamentally stupid we all are.

Down with the pavement.

I'm serious.

I know. That's why you're a freak.

Galen kept his focus on the pavement, walked a tight circle, around and around with a feeling that the center would melt, a great vortex that would pull him down. We're criminals, he said. Leaving her here.

Maybe you can get her to suck it.

Fuck you.

Not anymore. But I think Grandma would be into that. You could close those curtains and she could gum away at it and forget where she is.

What the fuck? Why are you like this?

You could come back an hour later and get it again, because she won't remember. You could do it all day. Jennifer laughed.

Galen walked away toward the glass doors, but he was only partway there when his mother emerged.

She shouldn't be here, he said. Even if she walks off and dies, it's better than being here.

His mother ignored him and walked past. She got in and started the car, and he knew she'd leave without him, so he slid into the passenger seat, damp from his grandmother.

What was the amount on that check? his mother asked as they pulled onto the road.

It was enough, Helen said.

How much?

None of your business.

Well, I just want you to know this. I don't want to see you or Jennifer ever again.

That's not a problem.

I mean that. Not ever again. You are never to show up at the house again.

Like I said, that's not a problem. It was the plan, in fact.

Yeah, Jennifer said. We already talked about it.

But the reason I'm telling you is in case that check doesn't work out for you. If the check doesn't work out, you're going to want to come to the house.

The check will work.

But if it doesn't, here's the deal. If I ever see you again, you get nothing. But if you stay away, I'll get Mom to write checks for Jennifer for college each semester.

Galen pounded the dashboard with his fist. So angry he couldn't speak. He felt that if he spoke, he would hit his mother instead of the dashboard.

I'm not paying for anything expensive. Just a state school, but I'll get Mom to write those checks if I never have to see you again.

Galen punched his own thighs. He was afraid of what he could do. He folded his arms in tight and closed his eyes and tried to just get through the time. Trapped here right next to her.

The figs ripe. Hot still air thick with their scent. Galen in the tree pushing at a fig with both hands until its purple skin burst open in a seam, exposed, and he sucked at the meat, delicious fruit. The stickiness all over his face and hands.

Galen knew he was eating to cover his grief. He would never see Jennifer again. It felt as if a section of his chest had been removed, and in its place, a gravity hole becoming increasingly dense, an impossible weight.

He wrapped his legs tight around a limb, hung beneath it and walked out the limb with his hands, strung himself as far as he could to reach two figs, enormous and heavy, their bodies hot and slack from the sun. So ripe inside the skin had become translucent.

Galen, his mother called.

He thought of not answering. If he just never answered again, what would happen then?

Galen, she repeated. She'd come out the back door onto the lawn, carrying a tray of finger sandwiches.

Not the finger sandwiches, he said.

There you are, she said, but it didn't sound the way it usually did. No delight in her voice, as there'd been only a few days ago, before the cabin. It sounded more now like she'd located a target.

I'm having figs for lunch, he said.

I have something to tell you.

Well I can hear from up here.

She set the tray down on the wrought-iron table. Galen could see the table's leaf pattern, and it seemed lovely to him for the first time. Heavy and old, but lovely.

I've made a decision, she said.

I can't wait to hear.

You were all my world once upon a time, she said. You really were. I wanted a baby. I don't know why. And if I could go back now and make it never have happened, I certainly would. But for a time there, having a baby was a magical thing.

Thanks, he said. For that part about wanting to go back.

Shut up and listen. I'm giving you a gift right now. I'm letting you know the whole thing.

Galen wanted to scream, but he felt a little afraid, too, so he only readjusted lower on the limb, found a more comfortable position in a vee with one of the main trunks. Holding the two figs in one hand.

I saw the world opening. I'm not sure what I saw, exactly, or how I could have believed any of it, but maybe it was something like imagining how we'd play in the walnut orchard, playing tag through the trees. Yellow mustard and wildflowers, and laughter. Maybe something like that, from the best moments of my own childhood in the orchard.

She wasn't looking at him. She was gazing off into the orchard, and she had her teacup held in both hands, but just floating there, not drinking from it.

This is sounding like an after-school special, he said.

You want to make everything small. That's what you've done.

You've tried to make everything small. But I'm going to continue on anyway, because this is important to me. It's important to me to let you know, just this once.

Fine, he said.

There was some feeling about it, some feeling about you. It was that Christmas-morning feeling, something really as innocent and pure as that. What I imagined was joy. And I think what I wanted, really, was to remake my own childhood. I wanted to go back and fix everything and live it the way it should have been.

His mother still hadn't looked at him. It was disconcerting.

There was supposed to be a man. And I thought I had found that man, but when I told him I was pregnant, I watched everything just fade and die. It was less than a minute. It really was that fast. Everything he had felt for me just went away.

Who was he?

He lost that chance. He doesn't get to be named or have anything told about him except the one part that matters, that he let everything just die in less than a minute. That's all you need to know about him.

That's real helpful. The daddy-minute. It explains so much.

It explains everything. It explains the truth about men, the truth that they care only about themselves. And you're no different. I thought maybe you'd be different. That's what I hoped.

This is all such self-serving crap. You should fucking listen to yourself.

That's right. Straight to the fuck words. All violence. That's who men are.

Fuck you.

Yeah. Fuck your mother. A favorite insult. But I'm not letting you take this away from me. I'm here to tell you a story.

Once upon a time.

That's right. Once upon a time. Because it was a fairy tale. I believed you could be good.

Galen hated this conversation so much.

I spent all my time with you. All my time, for years. I helped you learn each word. Just think about that for a minute. I helped you learn every single word that you know.

Galen tried to focus on his exhales, tried to calm.

I helped you learn every sound. How an *s* sounds, how a *z* sounds. How a *p* is different from a *b*.

Well thanks, Galen said. If that's what you're looking for, thanks for all the instruction.

Shut up. You need to listen. Today you only listen.

Fuck that.

You're going to listen today, because I've made a decision, and you need to know what this decision is. And I want you to really understand it. I want you to know why I made it.

Well let's just get to it, then. What's the decision?

No. I want you to understand first.

Fuck me.

That's right. Look at it however you need to. But shut up and let me finish.

Fine. Do tell.

Where was I? She put her teacup down, put her palms flat on the table, looking at her hands. Okay. I watched how every expression developed. How you laughed and forgot to laugh, how you smiled and how that smile twisted up and changed, how your temper and crying became your anger, although I have to admit, I don't really understand your anger. Your anger is something foreign, something I can't see coming. Your anger is part of how you're no longer mine.

So you're only claiming the good parts?

No. I'm just tracing things. And there's a gap there. And it's the gaps that make you someone I can't be with anymore.

Is that the decision?

No. It's related. Maybe it is the decision, actually. Maybe that's the fundamental thing, that I just don't want you in my life anymore, but it's not the decision I need to tell you about now.

Well about fucking time.

There's more I need to explain. I haven't even started, really. Because you're going to be angry, and you're going to feel betrayed, and you're going to believe it's unfair, and you're going to think it's about me and not about you. But I want you to understand. And I need you to know that it really is about you.

This is driving me crazy. You really are crazy.

No I'm not. And you won't call me crazy again.

Crazyland, Galen said. That's where you've lived for a while now. Look at you with your fucking afternoon tea and sandwiches. Think for a second about who else plays make-believe all day. Who is it who plays make-believe all day?

I'm not going to let you distract me.

Think about it. Children play make-believe all day, but who else does that? What adults do that, and where do they all live together?

Galen's mother looked up at him finally. That's been your gift to me, she said. To call me crazy.

The nut farm. You grew up on one kind of nut farm, but now you're ready to live in a different kind of nut farm. Galen liked this idea, but he stopped, because he didn't really like to see his mother hurt. That was always the problem. She deserved to be treated worse, but he could never do it.

I'm going to live right here, she said. But you're not.

Is that the decision?

No.

Throwing me out on the street, like you were threatening at the cabin? Even though you've been taken care of your whole life?

Let me continue, she said. I'm trying to tell you that I loved you. I loved you your whole life, and I tried.

You were my mother. That's what you were supposed to do.

You don't understand anything.

No one made you have me.

She shook her head. I'm not going to let you do this to me.

Yeah, because I'm doing such awful things to you right now. I'm the one making threats, saying I've made some kind of life-changing decision.

I tried even when you became like this, even when everything you did was ugly. I tried to still love you. I tried to forgive you. I tried to let you become whatever you needed to become, even if that meant you lived at home all your life.

Like you have.

Let me finish.

You don't get to finish if everything you say is crazy. I only have to listen if what you say is reasonable. I don't have to listen if it's crazy talk.

I hate you. I hate you so much.

Fine, he said. He dropped his two figs and climbed down out of the tree. That's great. You're a great mother. You've really improved on things from your past, just like you wanted to.

Galen's mother was crying without sound, in great hiccups of breath. She could hardly speak. I shouldn't hate my own child, she said. I know that. But I hate you.

Well you won't have to see me anymore. I'm moving out to the room above the shed.

Galen's mother began to smile. It was the strangest thing. She was still crying, but she began to smile. She sucked in breath, and what she did was laugh. Instead of crying, she was laughing at him.

What? he asked.

You don't understand, she said. You have no idea.

Well stupid me, then. You've been so clear.

She was smiling. You think you can just move out to the shed, and that's going to be it.

Yeah. I'm moving to the shed. You're not going to see me, but you're going to give me money for school and food and other things, too. You're going to stop fucking up my life.

The shed is not where you're going, she said.

I'm moving my stuff right now. He began walking toward the house.

You're going to prison.

Galen stopped. He had this feeling of heat rising all through him. Did you just say prison?

Yes. Prison.

How am I going to prison?

Statutory rape.

That's ridiculous.

Your cousin is seventeen. You're twenty-two. Even if she weren't your cousin, it would be statutory rape. And since she's your cousin, it may be incest, also. We'll have to see.

This is too stupid. I'm not even talking about this. This is what I mean by crazyland. He kept walking toward the house, and it seemed farther than before. It felt like the lawn fell away to either side of him. He was left to walk on a kind of narrow bridge of lawn to the pantry door, and then he was inside the house and safe. He walked quickly through the kitchen to the stairs and up to his room, where he took the duffel that was still packed and hefted it over his shoulder.

His mother was on the stairs. I'm going to be the witness, she said. And I brought the top blanket, the blanket that has both of you on it. I brought that as evidence.

You collected evidence?

That's right. So even if you and she both deny it, I have evidence. And you haven't had a shower, so you're evidence, also. And she hasn't had a shower.

You're insane.

I just want you to know that I've loved you all your life, but I have to stop you now. I have to do the right thing. And I have to let you know, also, that I can't visit you in prison. I can't go there. I can't have that become a part of my life.

You've thought about this.

Yes.

You've thought about it all the way up to me being in prison and you not visiting.

Yes. I almost drove us all to the police station, after we dropped off Grandma. But I decided I wanted to explain to you. I want you to understand. That's my gift to you.

The house felt to Galen like a cavern. No lights on, shades drawn. Great hollows in the ceiling above. Prison. His life, not someone else's life. His life in prison. And for doing nothing wrong.

Please, he said. I don't understand this. I don't know how this happened. He had to be careful how he talked to her. She really was crazy. I can't go to prison, he said. You're my mother.

Yes. I'm your mother. And that's why I have to do this. It's my responsibility.

Please. Please think about this. You're talking about prison.

Yes.

You're talking about sending your own son to prison.

Yes.

She had a strange attentiveness, something he couldn't place at first, and then he realized what it was. She was excited. You're excited, he said.

Yes. I guess I am. It's been so long. I've been afraid of you for so long. But now I won't have to see you ever again. I get my life back.

You can't just throw people away.

You threw yourself away.

Please. I'm your son.

She turned away then, walked down the stairs and toward the kitchen.

Where are you going?

She didn't answer, but there was a phone in the kitchen. He dropped his duffel and went after her fast. The light in the kitchen was on, and she was already reaching for the phone.

No! he yelled.

Her hand jerked back as she saw him coming after her. She screamed and ran out the pantry door.

He followed her onto the lawn, but she was already across it, running for the shed.

What the fuck are you doing, Mom? he yelled. I'm your son. I'm not some kind of monster.

She disappeared around the corner, and he just stood there on the lawn. Prison. He couldn't believe any of this. None of it could possibly be real. But it felt real. It felt more real than anything else ever had before. The world did not seem like an illusion. His mother was going to call the police. That had an enormous and terrifying reality.

Galen's life closing in around him. The shed, the old house, the trees above, the walnut orchard, all of it edging in closer. The end of a future. To have no future at all.

I'm not garbage, he yelled. I'm not something you can just throw away.

The air so hot and thick. He walked through it past the corner of the shed, into the orchard and around to the sliding bay door. It was closed. He stood there before it in the hot sun and begged. Please, he said. Please. I'll go away. You won't have to see me. But I can't go to prison. I don't even know what prison is.

He got down on his knees in the dirt, in the broken furrows. Please, he begged. Please.

He could feel the heat radiating from the old wood and from the ground. His body slick. He crawled closer and reached up for the handle. I'm just coming in to talk, he said. I just want to talk. But she'd somehow locked the door. It wouldn't slide.

He stood up and pulled harder, but it wouldn't budge. The old rusted handle, the old padlock hanging. It didn't have a lock inside. But she must have jammed a piece of wood or something.

Please, he said. Let me in. We need to talk.

I'll give you a head start. If you leave now, I'll give you one hour before I call.

No. I don't want one hour. You can't do this, Mom. He slumped against the door, old gray wood, rough and weathered and hot against his cheek.

The unfairness was too much. Rape. It couldn't be called rape. I'm not a rapist, he said.

She didn't answer. Just waited there in the shed, the place of her childhood. Her childhood that was so special and couldn't be touched by anyone else. The whole thing a lie.

I'm not a rapist.

You are a rapist, and an abuser. And you will never abuse me again.

What the fuck? He slapped the wood with his open palm.

See?

You're crazy.

See?

You stop fucking saying that.

See?

Galen was so frustrated he yelled and kicked at the door.

You're an animal, she yelled at him. You're an animal, and you deserve to live in a cage.

Galen stepped back and turned to kick at the door with the heel of his shoe. He kicked it hard. But it was tougher than it looked. I'll show you some fucking abuse, he said. If you're going to use that word, then you should learn what it means.

You're just giving me more to say in court. I'll tell them you tried to kill me.

Galen stopped kicking. He couldn't believe any of this. She kept twisting things around. He needed to think. He needed to think his way out of this.

Look, he said. Let's calm down. Let's think about this. I never hurt you. I'm not an abuser. Can we agree on that, at least?

You're an abuser.

Galen couldn't stay here. He was going to just scream if he stayed here. He needed to go away for a while and calm down and think. But he couldn't have her calling the police while he did that.

There was a bar that fit over the door handle. He swung this in place and then tried to close the padlock. It was rusty and didn't close easily, but he brought a thigh up to hold the bottom of it and he pushed down with both hands until it locked.

What are you doing?

I closed the padlock. I have to think for a while. I have to figure this out. And I can't have you calling the police.

She laughed. That's perfect. You're hanging yourself.

Are you my mother? he screamed. He screamed so hard his throat hurt, the same as when he vomited, his mouth and throat stretched wide open and burning. Are you my mother?

creaming at her like that made him weak. Everything gone inside, a hollow. It wasn't even anger. It was something far more desperate, the entire world unmoored. He walked toward the house reduced to a shell. There was nothing left at all.

The blanket was somewhere in the house, and he would find it. Not that finding it would make much difference.

Her room a child's room still. Wooden toys from Germany on the shelves, wagons and nutcrackers and small wooden girls. A full-size rocking horse also out of wood. Everything placed carefully, the most special of her childhood remembrances.

He didn't really understand who his mother was. He hadn't been there when she was made, or lived any of the years when she was remade. He didn't have anywhere to start from. And what she was doing now was unimaginable. The way they were talking to each other was unimaginable.

What happened? he asked aloud.

He found her small suitcase in the closet, but it was empty, already unpacked from the trip. He pushed dresses and coats aside, found paper bags of sweaters and socks. No sign of the blanket.

Her bed small, with a light blue cover. He knelt down, looked under the bed, and there it was. An old brown blanket from the cabin, and somewhere on it the signs of his crime.

Galen lay down on the wood floor and put the blanket under his head, a pillow. He just lay there because he didn't know what to do. He needed to undo things, to make them not have happened. Where had he and his mother first gone wrong?

The blanket was rough wool, very old. And this was the problem. Galen and his mother had gone wrong before Galen was even born. That was the truth. And it was outrageously unfair that he should be blamed now.

This is not me, he said. This is not even about me.

He rose and took the blanket into the backyard, dumped it on the lawn. Then he went to the kitchen for matches and returned to burn this blanket and everything it meant. He watched the flame start at one corner, nearly invisible in the sun. Hints of blue and orange. He could feel the warmth as the fire spread, warmer even than this hot sun, and he could see the wool turning black and thinning as it was consumed. The fire known by what it left behind.

The blanket shrank into a ball, knitted itself up tightly and blackened and then returned itself to earth and air, becoming ash and vapor, no more than a gray smudge against the green. This is what Galen needed to do somehow with his life. He needed to find some burning away, some regeneration, some promise to start fresh.

He washed himself in the shower, scrubbing mercilessly at his dick. There'd be no sign left of Jennifer. And no doubt she'd had three showers by now.

Galen took his underwear to the back lawn and burned that, too. Then he walked to the shed, stood before the door with its rusty lock.

I'm thirsty, she said. It's hot in here. You need to unlock that door and leave. I'll give you one hour.

I burned all of it.

What's that?

I burned the blanket. I burned my underwear. I took a shower. And you know Jennifer's had a shower already. So there's no evidence left.

It won't matter. I'm the witness, and that's what's important. How often does a mother testify against her own son? They'll believe me.

Why are you doing this?

Why did you become who you are?

Not like I could help that.

Well it's the same for this now. It's not like I have another choice.

You need to talk to me. You can't just talk like that.

I don't need to do anything.

This isn't even about me.

That's what I was saying. I knew you'd think this wasn't about you. I knew you'd feel it was just my problem and a betrayal and unfair. But I need you to know this really is about who you are. You're an animal, and you deserve to spend the rest of your life in prison.

Mom. Galen didn't know what else to say. I'm not an animal.

You are an animal.

The sun so hot. He walked around the corner to the small toolshed, built off the wall of the main shed. It would be shady in there. He swung open the wooden door and was reminded of his grandfather. The tools rarely used now, but his grandfather had been in here all the time, always working on the orchard or hedge or buildings when he wasn't at work as an engineer. His entire life had been work. And that should have made him a good man, but he beat his wife, and because of that he would never be a good man. He was an abuser. That's what the word meant.

And everyone in the family screwed up because of it. He was the one who should have been locked away. Galen had done nothing wrong. His mother was blaming him for her father. She was sending her father to prison.

I'm not your father, he said, loud enough for her to hear through the wall.

Where are you?

I'm in the toolshed. And I'm not your father.

Why are you in the toolshed?

It's shady in here. It's hot, and there's nowhere to sit, but at least it's not in the sun.

Well it's hot in here. You have to unlock the door and leave. I'm tired of waiting. I need to get out of here, and I need something to drink.

You're trying to send your father to prison. That's what's happening.

This is about you.

Galen picked up a shovel and smacked the wall. It was a big shovel, heavy, with a wide flat blade, not rounded.

What are you doing?

He smacked it again, started a rhythm.

Stop that.

I'm going to keep doing this until you admit this is all about your father and not about me.

Stop it right now.

But Galen kept hitting the wood with the shovel, a steady rhythm, getting the face to hit as flat as possible for the loudest smack. Leaning over the smaller tools to get to the wall. Pruners and hedge clippers and small garden shovels, tools accumulated over decades. The shovel heavy very quickly, his shoulders burning and his breath ragged, but he kept going.

She had stopped talking, and that was good.

Galen wished he had used a smaller shovel. He didn't want to interrupt the rhythm, but finally he just couldn't hold it up anymore.

Keep going, she said.

He walked out into the sun and just wandered through the orchard, bareheaded and sun-crazed, the heat moving in heavy bands around him. The furrows uneven and clodded, unturned for years now. The irrigation system still working, thin dark tracks along the rows of trunks, evaporating. He took off his shoes and squished into the mud, cooling his feet at least. The shade here still hot, sunlight everywhere through the leaves, no real shade. The walnuts a brutal tree.

In the heat and bright noon sun, the trunks seemed farther apart, the orchard expanded, just like metal.

He moaned and growled for a while and walked aimlessly through the dirt. When his feet got too hot, he stepped in mud and then roved on. Weeds and stickers, every single plant unfriendly. Most of them looked dead, but they were still standing upright, thin brown and yellow stalks of crap bush and shitty weed and fuck grass. Years of dead and dried leaves decayed, a layer of skins. And where the dirt still showed, even the brown had been bleached out of it. Dirt become more white than brown. This desolate place. Great for the grasshoppers and bees and butterflies, the grasshoppers the worst, the sound of their landings all around him. He went after a few, stomped on them as they landed, smashed them in his hands, crunchy brown bodies, oversize heads with big black eyes watching him, legs too thin to be made of anything. What he wanted was for all of them to die and just take the weeds with them, clear out the orchard, and then he wanted some rain. He wanted the dirt to be brown again, and he wanted the sun to stop.

One parent, he said. I get one parent in life, and this is it. This is what I get. He walked to the far fence, a high fence the new sub-division had put up, twice as tall as he was, made of cinder blocks painted an orange-brown to blend in. The houses the same color, the top part of their second stories protruding. The racket of their air conditioners running all day and night. Another kind of prison, living in that subdivision, but nothing like the prison he had coming.

He couldn't even think of it. He couldn't see himself in a prison. That was not something his brain was willing to do. That was not a picture that could make any sense. It was like standing on the moon in a T-shirt and shorts, or lounging in a chair on Mars, having tea.

Galen felt dizzy from the heat, so light-headed, he walked over and sat against a trunk. The shade a kind of punishment. A re-minder of shade without being the real thing, the walnut leaves not dense enough in this sun. They had grown more thickly before, when the trees were pruned and taken care of. They had dead branches now, and produced less walnuts, and were ragged looking.

Lemonade, he said. I need some lemonade. So he got up and walked all the way across the orchard, another moon mission, and said nothing to his mother as he passed the shed. He crossed the lawn and into the house and made a big pitcher, a glass pitcher with a glass stirrer, a long clear shaft with a clear bulb on the end. It made a nice sound as he stirred, and he added lots of ice so that would clink around. He was making lemonade from a mix, and he didn't add fresh lemons as his mother usually did, but it tasted fine.

He brought the lemonade on a tray with two glasses to the table under the fig tree.

Galen? his mother asked.

Yep.

You let me out of here right now.

Sorry, he said. I'm busy. He pulled a chair closer to the shed wall, moved the table over. The shade here from the fig tree was perfect.

Huge leaves, an old enormous tree, and none of it was dying. It was in the peak of health. He poured himself a glass, then he asked her, would you like a glass too?

What?

I just poured myself a glass of lemonade. Would you like a glass too?

Yes.

Okay then. He poured her a glass. There you go, he said.

That's cruel.

It is what it is. You're the one hiding in the shed. Safe in your special place. If you want the lemonade, then come out and get it.

He had a drink of the lemonade. Ah, he said. That's good. I was really thirsty. It's a scorcher today.

He could hear the shed door rattled and slammed, but muffled since it was far away on the other side.

Galen! his mother screamed.

That's abuse, he said. Try to rein in that anger. Come and just sit and have a glass of lemonade and we'll talk. We're both reasonable here.

I'm going to tell them you tried to kill me. I'm going to tell them you locked me in here.

You locked yourself in.

Your fingerprints will be on that lock.

Yeah, he said, and tilted the glass. He closed his eyes and tried to focus on the lemonade, cold and sweet and bitter, also. He didn't know how they had arrived at this moment, him sitting under the fig tree alone, his mother locked in the shed, sending him to prison. None of it was possible. I don't understand how we got here, he said.

You raped your cousin. That's pretty simple.

If you keep saying that, how can I let you out?

You let me out right now.

You know what I imagine when I imagine prison?

Walk around the shed right now and unlock this door.

What I imagine is standing on the moon in a T-shirt and shorts. That's what I just imagined, when I was out there in the orchard.

If you don't unlock this, you'll get more than prison. You'll get the death sentence.

It's the moon, but the air is fine, and the temperature is fine. It's really quiet, and there's no wind. There's only rock and dark sand stretching as far as I can see, and I know that this is it. This is all I get. I'll never see another person. I'll never see another color except the color of this rock and sand.

Prison is not the moon.

I know. What I'm saying is that I can't imagine prison. I can't even imagine it. I can't go there.

You're going there.

But that's the thing. I'm not going there.

Yes you are.

Fine, he said. He stood up and grabbed the glass pitcher. He stepped to the wall and poured the lemonade against a wide plank. There's your lemonade, he said. Enjoy.

I'm telling them all of this. They're going to hear every detail. How you tortured me.

Torture, he said. Now I'm a torturer. Is there anything you're not willing to call me?

I'm not willing to call you my son.

Galen laughed. That's great. That's great. Thanks, Mom. You're a hell of a mom. Thanks for really being there for me.

Galen. You need to understand this. Every minute that you keep me in here makes it worse for you.

Mom. You need to understand this. You're locked in a fucking shed.

Galen lay on his bed staring into the dark caverns of his ceiling. Like craters, his own moonscape right here all along. Sunspots floating around his eyes still, solar flares. His mother another planet, far away, twisting and twisting. The two of them locked into some kind of orbit together.

The air cool in here, even without air-conditioning. Old house, thick walls, thick roof, heavy insulation and heavy drapes. A kind of fortress against the valley.

Galen closed his eyes, and the sunspots did not link up into any pattern. Rounded blurs floating and vanishing, moving suddenly to new regions, like UFOs. Able to appear and disappear in a wink.

He liked the idea of standing on the moon. The light would be always at a slant, like evening on earth, right before sunset, except the sun would never go all the way down. Long shadows trailing from every rock, shadows even in the large grains of sand. A presence to everything, luminous, and no other human. No tracks. He would always know that he was standing on the surface of an orb. He'd be able to feel that, the curvature wrapping away on every side. And when he walked, his feet would touch what had never been touched before. He'd go barefoot and feel the slight coolness of the surface, uniform and unchanging, every rock and grain of sand equalized for billions of years in the unchanging sun. Each step of his would be older than any dinosaur's, disrupting sand arranged in an earlier era, broken and sifted in the time when planets were made, when the moon was ripped from the earth.

Going back. That would be the greatest gift. If he could go back even a few days, his mother would not be in the shed.

He tried to think of a way out of this situation. What she had said was true. Every minute was making things worse for him. He was more trapped than she was.

The inside of Galen's mind was just empty. There was no direction he could go. So he sat up, walked downstairs and onto the lawn. She was yelling. He hadn't heard anything from inside the house.

Help! she was yelling. Help me! Someone help me! All of it muffled. She was inside a box. She was banging at the walls.

Galen walked closer, tried to figure out where she was banging and what she was using. She wasn't at the back wall by the fig tree, and not on the side wall either. He walked into the orchard and could see the sliding door flexing and shaking a little as she pounded.

What are you doing? he asked.

You're going to swing for this, she said, and then she continued yelling. Help me! I'm in the shed!

No one can hear you.

Someone will hear me. And they're going to drag you like a dog and put chains on you.

Well that's a nice thought. Thanks, Mom. But where are these people coming from? I couldn't hear you even from inside the house. Think about how far away the nearest neighbor is. And they all have their air conditioners running, for another two months at least.

You can't get away with this.

I'm not getting away with anything. You're the one who made all this happen. This is your show.

You won't get away with it.

I didn't do anything.

Trying to kill your own mother. You know how a jury is going to look at that. Trying to kill your own mother.

You! he screamed. *You* put yourself in the shed! *You* put yourself in the fucking shed! He slammed the door with his hand, slammed it over and over. Goddamn you!

If I had known who you'd become, I would have killed you. Just a hand over your nose and mouth when you were a baby. It would have been so easy.

What you're not understanding is that you have to help me figure out how to let you out of the shed. That's what you're not understanding. And when you talk about putting me in chains or killing me, that doesn't give me a great reason to let you out.

I'm not making a deal with you.

Yes you are.

You're going to prison. Nothing is going to change that.

Goddamn it. I'm not going to stand here talking with you like this. It's too fucking hot. How about you sit in there for a day and then we'll talk again.

You let me out right now.

Yeah, I'll get right on that. He walked around to the shade of the fig tree and could hear her banging at the walls. It sounded like she was throwing the walnut racks.

He sat down at the table and felt thirsty. The afternoon promising to stretch on forever, and the air was not going to cool. It would only become more dense, piling up over time, the heat melting and compacting it. What had been thirty feet of air was becoming five feet of air, unbreathable.

He needed some lemonade, so he went into the house, made another batch, didn't have any ice this time but the water was cool enough. The air in here so much more breathable. He went for a handful of chocolate chips in the pantry, a treat, and saw saltine crackers and grabbed a packet of them. An inspiration.

I made lemonade again, he said. And I brought you some food.

She was whacking at the side wall.

He had the chocolate chips in his hand still, melting, turning his palm brown, and he dropped them, leaned down and wiped his hand on the overgrown grass. Too sweet.

I said I have lemonade, he said a little louder. And I brought some food.

She stopped whacking. Galen, she said. She sounded out of breath. I can't do this. You need to open the door. Her voice muffled, and he didn't know exactly where she was, somewhere there in the darkness and he was blinded here in the light.

I'd be happy to.

Well do it now then.

I have to know I'm not going to prison.

You're going to prison.

Galen opened the white plastic packet of saltines, went to the wall, and slipped crackers in through the gaps in the planks. Here's your food, he said. This is all the food you're getting for the next day, so be careful with it.

This will be perfect. When I tell them I was dying of thirst in the heat and you fed me saltines.

The thing is, you're not telling the story yet. You're not standing in court. You're still living the story. And that's your food for the next day.

He slipped a dozen crackers through the planks and heard her come up close. She slammed the wall where he was standing and then pushed crackers out the bottom gap between ground and wall. It was a small gap, no more than an inch high, but Galen noticed it suddenly. The entire shed built on posts buried into the ground, and the planks came down almost to the ground but weren't buried. She could dig her way out pretty quickly anywhere along the wall.

Fuck, he said.

What's that?

Nothing. He walked all the way around to the toolshed, grabbed one of the smaller rounded shovels, and wondered where to start. It would be best if he could just follow her. If she started digging, he'd throw dirt back in that area. But that meant he'd have to stay awake. Even an hour or two of sleep and she could get out. Which meant he should start now and mound up enough dirt everywhere along the edge.

If he started shoveling, though, she'd know. And she hadn't started digging yet. Maybe it would never occur to her. He couldn't believe he was having these thoughts.

We have to stop this, Mom, he said. We have to figure something out. This is too awful. This is not me.

This is you. This is who you've been all along. All your New Age crap, how you're an old soul. But you're a murderer. That's who you are.

Galen walked along the edge of the shed, walked the entire perimeter, gray wood reaching just short of the earth. The ground hard, untilled in close, and she had no tools, no shovel, so he doubted, really, that she could get very far, but it was hard to know. He'd become a jailor.

He found the largest gaps at the sliding door in front, so that was where he broke ground. The earth heavier than he had imagined. A shovelful a considerable thing. He had imagined before that the crust was so thin he could fall through and tumble to the other side of the planet, but now he wasn't so sure. The world an illusion, but what seemed paper-thin one moment could solidify the next. It was all changing constantly. The fact that Galen was shoveling may have increased the thickness of the earth right here. The illusion testing him, responding to his consciousness. As we walked around, the world making and remaking itself.

The point was the struggle. The earth thickened here so that he would labor. The shovel felt heavy so that he could feel he was doing something. The world provided resistance, and as we struggled through, we learned our final lessons.

The sound of the shovel entering the earth. That was a complex and beautiful sound, deceptively fast and not all of one piece at all. And the light thud and sifting of stones and clods and fine grains falling away as he lifted the shovel, that was a reminder that we were all made of this. Everything we knew was fragment. Streams held together to appear as solids. The fundamental nature of all things. And the thrill was in the fling, when he flung the shovelful against the old wood, against the gap, and he heard it hit in a thousand ways all masquerading as one sound, as one action.

Galen knew now that what was happening here was important. His mother locked in this shed was a gift. This was his final lesson. It was here that he would feel and know the impermanence of all things. Not just think it or suspect it but know it. This was his river. Galen had always looked to water, thinking his meditation would be the same as Siddhartha's, the water in which he would see all things forming and dissipating, but Galen's rightful meditation had been here all along, a meditation on dirt. He had grown up alongside it, had known it all his life but never recognized it. He lifted another shovelful and flung, the million tiny grains spraying outward into pattern and collapse, and he felt an incalculable joy, a thrill that ran right through him.

My god, he said. It was right here all along.

What are you doing? his mother asked, but he ignored her. She was only the catalyst. She had locked herself in here to draw his attention to this, to give him this meditation. That was the purpose of all of it, of all their fighting and struggle. But she wouldn't know. She wouldn't understand her role. She'd try to distract him.

Thank you, he said. I honor this gift.

What are you talking about?

It's okay that you don't know, he said. You're still locked in samsara. You're a younger soul.

I'm locked in the shed, because you locked me in here.

Galen lifted another shovelful, the shovel become lighter, the action smoother. He lifted and flung again, watched for pattern in the dirt as it was lofted through time and space.

Galen.

He was being lofted. He understood that now. He was the dirt. He was watching himself being flung.

What are you doing with the shovel?

Shh, he said. This is important. I can't have you as a distraction. I'm getting close here.

Hey! she yelled.

But he ignored her, plunged the shovel deep into the earth, powered now by a force that was beyond muscle and bone. He was becoming the action itself. He was the dirt, and the shovel, and the movement, but more than that. He was a million miles removed. These hands were not his hands. This breath was not his breath. This mother was not his mother. This Galen was not Galen. He had to let it all go, let the movement happen without attachment.

His mother's fingers at the gap between wood and earth, white fingers pushing away the dirt that was building, and more dirt lofted through air, through time, onto those fingers, buried and emerging again, a beautiful dance, a movement known forever and meant to be.

The earth deepening, building against the old wood, and her fingers moved to the side, at the edge of the mound, found a larger gap, the entire back of one hand showing, and more dirt lofted onto it, buried now, and another shovelful, and his mother was screaming, a sound become muffled, a sound transformed, a sound that was cradled between earth and air and rocked and buried and buried again.

This meditation became the longest of Galen's life, the most sustained, the most beautiful. The shovel into the earth, the swing, the dirt suspended in air and then falling, filling the gap between wood and untilled ground, the gap between human and earth, between past and present, self and truth. The old planks above becoming all that was transitory, pitted and weathering, meeting all that was permanent below, and the new dirt bridging the gap, dissolving distinctions.

His mother a constant sound, an accompaniment, an honoring of the movement. Her fingers in the gap, enforcing distinctions, trying to divide the world, then buried again, a constant progression through opposites. The clearing of the gap and then the filling, the vanishing.

Galen could feel his hands tearing, the hot blisters forming and then breaking and leaking and the raw pain in flashes but then it would fade again, and he remained far away, watched all of it, watched his breath. The heat become a dense layer around him, radiating from his skull especially, and he threw off his shirt, lost no more than a stroke or two and was back in the swing of the shovel, the movement. His skin bare to the sun now, and he could feel each individual ray like a dart through space and time, arrived from the origin of the world, the light not only of our sun but of all suns, finding his back now and piercing his skin, the heat and light-headedness and piercing a gift, not a distraction. They only increased his focus.

He wanted something to drink, but that would wait. That was only samsara, distraction, and what he was riding here was his final meditation. He would ride this one all the way out, all the way past this incarnation, past unnumbered incarnations, past all that would hold him back, if only he could hold on.

But that was pride. He needed to not think of the meditation as accomplishment. He needed to stop evaluating. He needed to remain focused on the dirt, each grain. The surface, whiter on top where it had been bleached by sun, darker beneath, the odd, broken shapes, rough faces. Each grain and clod and rock as the shovelful hung in the air, to see the position of each in relation to every other, to see the grid, the pattern, and then watch the collapse.

His soul had done this through many centuries already, watched entire lifetimes form and fade, watched other mothers come and go. How many lifetimes? It was more likely he went back millennia, not just centuries. He might have been there when the caves were painted almost twenty thousand years ago, might have painted many of the horses and bulls himself. The cave cool and damp, somewhere in France, the cave dark, a place others were afraid to go, and each day he visited with his torch, brought charcoal from the campfire for his art. And there was a young woman in the camp who noticed this, who looked up from berry-picking when he passed, and who eventually followed him into the cave.

Damn it, he said. This was supposed to be a meditation, not a porn show.

What? his mother said.

I'm not talking to you.

You're calling this a porn show? You're burying your mother and calling it a porn show?

Galen slammed the wall with the shovel. Shut the fuck up! he yelled. I'm not talking to you. You have no idea. You don't know a single fucking thing that's going through my head.

You said porn show.

Galen slammed the shovel against the wood over and over. The air around him on fire, and he was dizzy and drenched and seeing sunspots. His hands torn up. His shoulders so weak he dropped the shovel and stumbled around to the shade of the fig.

He sat in the cast-iron chair and slumped forward onto the table. He was breathing hard. The air had no oxygen in it.

You've called me crazy, she said, but let's think about this. It sounded like she was close against the back wall, only a few feet from him. Her voice was rough, hoarse from the yelling. You've locked your mother in a shed, and you're trying to kill her.

I'm not trying to kill you.

You're mounding up dirt all along the wall, some weird kind of burial, and you don't listen when she screams. And then you start talking about porn.

Who is she?

What?

You said I don't listen when she screams.

She is me.

Exactly. And who's crazy?

We could find you help.

I thought you wanted to send me to prison.

They have prisons that are also mental health facilities.

I can't listen to you, Galen said. I can't listen to you ever again. He walked away with his hands over his ears and went into the house, looked through the kitchen drawers for earplugs. She had some wax earplugs somewhere. All the old silver, real silver, an insanity right here in the kitchen. Everything about their lives was insanity. And what he was doing was cutting through that. He was the antidote. He would return to his meditation and not be distracted by her.

Every small thing from the last century had been saved in these drawers. Ancient rubber bands, metal thumbtacks, a wooden ruler, buttons and scraps of twine, nothing ever thrown away, everything saved just in case. Galen removed a drawer, releasing the catch at the back, and took it out to the lawn, dumped a small pile of things brown or metallic, things that hadn't seen the sun in many decades.

Then he went for another drawer, and another, and he dumped them all. He took the drawers not only from the kitchen but also from the pantry, hallway, and dining room. He left everything heavy, all dishes and silverware, but took every drawer full of random little shit and dumped it. No sign of earplugs, but this project had become something else anyway, a purging, a burning back into sanity, a burning away of the old and useless.

Here's your past, he said.

What? Her voice muffled. The shed not a great facilitator of conversation.

Here's your past, he said more loudly, and then he had an inspiration. Your photos, he said.

What are you doing to my photos?

Nothing yet, but I think they're about to join this pile. Everything can burn.

No. You leave my stuff alone, Galen.

You're welcome to come stop me whenever you'd like.

Galen!

He entered her room and just stood there and looked around. This was the last time he would see all her things, the last time her room would be her room, and that seemed worth taking a moment. He would try to remember what this had looked like.

Mom, he said. Mom. He was trying out the sound of that, the accumulation of all that made the illusion. This room was part of it, this room that pretended a past, that stretched all the way back through her childhood. It was all illusion but had a convincing weight. Everything from the time period: the old wooden toys, the clothing, even her childhood drawings on the walls, of a house and family, the four of them holding hands under an enormous sun. That distorted sun should have been the clue.

Her bookshelf had the photo albums. He grabbed two of the older ones, the white covers like faded linoleum, and walked out to the lawn.

Got a couple albums, he said. Memory lane.

Leave those alone.

Goats, he said. A lot of goats, right out here in the orchard, and you in your sundress.

I don't have copies of any of those, Galen.

The goats were looking at the camera, posing along with Galen's mother and aunt. His aunt older, much taller, and with no bow in her hair. She already looked unhappy. His mother smiling her cutest smile, performing, her head tilted a little to the side. You were kind of like Shirley Temple, he said.

Put those away, Galen.

Is that who you were trying to be? Is that who you're being now when you're all fake and weird?

Galen waited, but his mother didn't respond. Never mind, Galen said. I know you don't answer when it's anything real. The cute moments are a sacred thing that can't be talked about. He yanked the page out of the album and crinkled it, the layers of card stock and photo and thin plastic film.

No! she yelled. You stop that right now.

This is kind of fun. I like the shed. I can do whatever I like. I hope you have an eyeball stuck to one of the gaps between the planks so you can see all this. I'd hate for you to miss out.

You're worse than anything I could imagine, worse than anything I can say. I don't even have a name for you.

Try son. The word son might be a possibility. Here's a photo of the walnuts. The fucking walnuts, and all the drying racks laid out.

Put that away.

Grandma and Grandpa aren't that old here. I can almost imagine them having real lives, being people who weren't just born old.

Their lives were real.

I don't know, he said, but it does seem possible in this photo. The problem is that there are no answers to anything. Why did he beat her? Why did he work all the time? How did she lose her memory?

You're talking about entire lives. No one can explain an entire life.

Wow. You're talking with me about your parents, sort of. This is new.

I've always talked about them.

No you haven't. You've never said anything real about anything important.

Galen.

It's true. Why did he beat her?

He didn't beat her.

See?

None of it was the way you think it was.

Well then enlighten me.

We were a family.

No. That's one thing you were not. Because the word family

means something special to you, and your family has never fit that word. You know what's odd about this photo with the walnut racks?

No answer from his mother. What's odd, he continued, is that they're still working. They don't stop for the photo. They just kind of look up for a moment. But they're still bent over the racks. And the racks go on forever. That's what your father's life was like. Just work that stretched forever in all directions, work for work's sake, and nothing else. No family.

I was there, so I'm the one who knows. We were a family, and we didn't just work. Dad played the accordion, and Mom played the piano, and we'd sing songs together.

Grandma plays piano?

Yeah. Almost everything is something you don't know.

Okay. So let's say I want to believe in that family. I still have to get everything to fit. So why did he beat her?

Damn you. He didn't beat her.

Galen ripped the photo from the album and crinkled it up.

Stop! Her voice broke, ragged and spent.

Save your voice, he said. The photo's no loss. None of this happened, after all. He didn't beat her, and there was no family, and there were no drying racks, no walnuts.

Galen could hear his mother sobbing now, but he didn't care. He looked at the other photos and ripped them out, a page at a time.

Here you are with a new bicycle, he said, and he ripped out that page. Here you are with a dog. What was that dog's name again?

Schatze, she said, and this made her sob harder.

Just a dog, he said, and not much of a dog. Those legs are about three inches high. What kind of dog is that again?

A dachshund.

Yeah, that's right. What a mistake of a dog.

I loved Schatze.

What's the name mean again?

Mein Schatz is my treasure or dear one or my love.

Galen ripped the page out. Well there are a lot of photos of my love, but not after today.

I hate you.

Yeah, I know. We've already covered that. Time to move on to something new.

I'm your mother.

Covered that point, too.

You have to let me out.

And again the familiar ground. I had hoped to get through these albums before going for the earplugs, but I may have to get them sooner.

You're a monster.

Yeah yeah.

You're not my son.

Uh-huh. He looked at another photo of Schatze, by the Christmas tree. His mother in a holiday dress that looked thick, like it was made of velvet, maybe. And the tree huge, out in the main room that was two stories high. Tinsel and hundreds of ornaments and a star on top. A blanket of felt underneath, and all the presents, piles of presents. Schatze with his paws up on her, straining to lick her face, and she had both arms around him, was laughing and trying to get her face away from his tongue. It almost looked like what she said. He could almost imagine the family she was claiming. And maybe they had good times. Maybe the good times stretched on and became most of the time. Maybe the beatings and favoritism and fakery were only occasional, the exceptions to how their lives were. But he would never know. His mother couldn't be trusted, because she was trying too hard to protect and deny. His aunt couldn't be trusted because she was trying too hard to

destroy. And his grandmother couldn't remember. These photos
were too brief, only moments. They couldn't describe what a day
felt like, how all the hours of even one day moved along. And this
was all a distraction anyway, the deepest form of samsara, the belief
in belonging, the belief in being tied to a family and a place and
time. The final attachment, the one that was the foundation for the
illusion of self.

The crinkled pages looked almost like flowers, large and shiny, the whites and darks of the petals, enormous white carnations dyed with ink. Two albums made a bed of flowers much larger than the piles from the junk drawers.

I'm a gardener, he said. I'm planting a family. And once all the flowers have bloomed, I'm going to pour gasoline on them and light a match. And that will be freedom, finally.

You're a demon, she said.

You're not even religious.

I know. But you're a demon. You're a force for evil. You're not a person gone bad. You're something that had this in him all along. This is your nature.

You can't believe in evil if you don't believe in god.

I can see the truth. I can see what you are.

There is no evil. There is only progression through opposites.

You haven't even read Blake.

Who's Blake?

Blake is the one you're parroting with all this crap from Kahlil Gibran and others. If you'd gone to college, you'd know.

Galen walked over to the table, picked up one of the heavy cast-iron chairs, and flung it against the shed wall.

That fixed it, his mother said. You're no longer an uneducated dumbass.

Galen went into the house, grabbed the rest of her photo albums, and then just stood there in her room. He had let her distract him. He had found his meditation, finally, and look how quickly he had left it and become caught up in something else. This was the problem. She had an unbelievable power to throw him off, like a magnet next to a compass. She could destroy everything just by opening her mouth.

He let the photo albums drop onto the floor. He had to find the earplugs.

They weren't on her nightstand. He looked in her bathroom, in the mirror cabinet above the sink, and found a set of old ones, two dirty globs. He stuffed one into each ear, listening now to the inside of his own head, to his own blood and synapses, and that was where he needed to be. No more distraction. Without sound, she could no longer reach him.

He found gauze to wrap his raw hands, and he kicked things around in her closet looking for gloves, dumped the drawers of her dresser onto the floor, all her socks and underwear and bras and blouses and everything else, and still no gloves.

So he marched out to the shed, walked all the way around it to the small toolshed, and looked in there. No doubt she was saying things to him now, but he could hear nothing but the airspace in his own skull.

His eyes had to adjust after the bright sun, but he found a small shelf along one side, and here were the gloves. He picked a light cotton pair, dark with dirt and grease, and smashed them in his hands to kill any black widows. Then he slipped them on over the gauze. He was going to commit to the meditation now.

He walked out front to the shed door, stood at the orchard edge with the trees to his back and looked at the dirt he'd mounded along the wall. It was a furrow, he realized now. He was extending the orchard, connecting it to the shed, cultivating something.

The trees at his back a kind of audience. They seemed full of expectation. Grown heavy out of the soil and hanging now in the air, waiting.

Okay, he said. I'm doing it. And he walked to the corner, where he had only a few feet of wall left. He plunged the shovel and his hands stung. His arms and back sore as he lifted. He'd already cramped up.

The dirt seemed only dirt, nothing more. It looked and felt and smelled like dirt. The shovel heavy, and the fling too weighted, no fling at all, no suspension to it, only a brutal gravity.

Come on, he said. He knew that all meditations began this way, uninspired, thick as clay, without connection. A transition from the unalert world to the alert one, a journey through the full thickness of appearance. A kind of burial and trying to dig oneself out, and it always felt impossible. Every time, every single time, it felt as if the thickness would never end, as if the world would never shift again, never slip, never transform and become.

He was burning, his entire neck and back and arms cooked at the surface, but even that was no transformation. Even that was dead and heavy. It only hurt. And his breath was ragged. He was tired.

His back hurt so much he didn't feel he could bend over any longer, but he kept going anyway, kept shoveling, took out the ear-plugs and tried to listen to the streams of dirt and rock falling off the sides of the shovel, sounding almost like water, and then the heavy *whump* as he dumped each load. The sharper sound of small rocks hitting wood when he aimed high. He was on the east wall now, partly in shade, working his way toward the lawn. The cool of the shade a beautiful thing.

What he liked most was the lofting, the moment all that dirt hung in the air. He remembered now that had been his focus in the earlier meditation.

The day passing, no longer an oven here in the shade, and the halo of heat around his head had broken. The alert world returning. But then he hit harder ground.

He didn't want to lose his momentum, but he'd hit the edge of the tilled orchard, hit solid earth, and he couldn't dip his shovel in and swing. The tip of the shovel buried only a couple inches, and when he pulled up, he had almost nothing. The ground like armor, with bits of rock in it, all compacted.

So he walked around to the other side, near the toolshed, baking in full sun. A slick all over his body instantly, the wall and ground radiating. He was able to dip his shovel deep into loose ground, pulled up and lofted, focused everything on the feel of that, studied that moment with each shovelful, felt his own body travel through suspension and fall.

Siddhartha had endured days, months, years in meditation, had sat at the water's edge and waited, but Galen had found a meditation in action, a much faster form. It was a gift he should share with others. He should perhaps write his own book of meditation, to leave as a sign, as a trail of bread crumbs, or perhaps he would skip that and go right to poetry. He had seen what others hadn't yet seen, and so even a simple description of his experience would be a poem.

He could see all the people lining up to meet him, not only at bookstores and libraries but even here at the house. The line stretching all the way down the hedge lane once they found out where he lived. They'd be out here shoveling, and it would take a bulldozer to flatten the dirt each day.

Damn it, he said. Stop thinking. Just shovel. Just dig and throw and watch the dirt. That's it. That's all there is.

There's me, too, his mother said, so he stuffed the earplugs back in.

The dirt had become dirt again and nothing more. Just heavy, and the day had been passing but now it had stalled again.

Fine, he said, and he dropped the shovel, but then he picked it up again because he remembered there was a purpose to all of this. It wasn't just a meditation. He was also mounding up dirt so she couldn't dig out.

His skin felt itchy. He was hot and burned and itching all over, having to stop to scratch at his arms and armpits and belly and back and crotch. All the sweat in different layers. Jennifer would never do this.

He threw his shovel, just flung it into the orchard. There was no way to get his mind to steady and focus, no way to leave thought behind. He was thinking of Jennifer now, and that would go on until he jacked off, he knew. That was the only thing that could stop it.

So he trudged around the shed across the lawn past the pile of crap that he'd already forgotten about, something he needed to burn later, and went up to his room, grabbed a *Hustler*, and walked into his mom's room. He was so dirty, he didn't want to lie down on his own bed, and she wouldn't be needing hers. It was all going out to the pile to burn anyway. He'd be taking her blankets and sheets out there and her pillow and even the mattress. Everything was going to burn until this room was bare. It was going to be only wood and wallpaper.

He dropped his shorts and underwear, and his crotch looked so white against the sunburned, dirt-covered rest of him. A boner already just from thinking about Jennifer and the *Hustler*. The opening at the tip like an eye, watching him, knowing everything about him, all his secrets, everywhere his thoughts had gone.

He took off the cotton glove, unwrapped the gauze, and his hand stung. It really hurt in the open air, the broken, exposed blisters. He tried grabbing on to his boner, but he couldn't use his full palm. Only thumb and fingers, but it was hard to do much that way. It wasn't very satisfying.

But he did his best. The man in the *Hustler* had just arrived in town, thirsty and with a boner. Even his horse had a boner. It was eyeing the camera.

This man wore spurs and stood at the bar downing a whiskey while a woman in red petticoats blew him. The man hardly noticed. Then she was bent over a table, and this was where Galen focused. High heels and fishnet stockings and legs spread, exposed and waiting, looking back to see what was coming. This was what Galen wanted. He'd never had Jennifer from behind. Something about this position was just more exciting than any other. He closed his eyes and tried to see her like that, tried to see what she'd look like in this dress. They'd get a small place out in the desert somewhere, let the dust blow in and cover the floor, and he'd wear spurs and bend her over an old wooden table. He'd drink a whiskey while he did it.

Galen had to grab on with his full palm. Otherwise it just wouldn't work. His hand stung terribly and his mother's bed was too springy. He was bouncing around, which was distracting. It was kind of weird, also, to be jacking off in his mother's bed. He felt like she was watching, almost, so he opened his eyes and expected her to be standing right there, but she wasn't. He was in here alone. He needed to focus and come and get this over with and get back to his meditation.

He was all distracted now, though, and he felt tired, incredibly tired. It had been a long day, far too long, starting at the cabin with breakfast and his mother rushing them out of there. Everything that had happened since had been insane, totally insane.

He had to look at the magazine again, at the woman spread over the table, and then at the man riding her from behind, drinking another whiskey. The man wasn't even looking at her. He was looking up at the ceiling. He was the man who had never seen anyone he'd done. It was distracting. Galen closed his eyes again and tried to remember what it had felt like inside Jennifer, silky he remembered, hot and tight and wet and he sped up his hand and went full tilt, did his best to make himself come, but his hand hurt and he couldn't focus and finally he gave up.

Fuck, he said. I can't come, and I can't stop thinking about sex. This is hell. His hand was throbbing in pain.

He curled on his side on his mother's bed and rested. Eyes closed, his breath heavy, just a few minutes of rest and then he'd go finish shoveling. His chest falling in great exhales, so much more exhausted than he'd thought, and he was sinking. He tried to rise up out of it, but somehow that made him fall even deeper.

An enormous grassland, and Galen walking. The earth volcanic, dark pumice covered in lichen. The yellow grass very sharp, growing in tufts like spines, growing from the rock itself.

Heat waves visible in the yellow and black and red, making mirages. Lone trees and cacti always at a distance, no shade. His feet and legs were not flesh and blood. They were more like pencil erasers, wearing down. As he walked, he was becoming gradually shorter, and so he had to hurry. He had to cross before he ran out of eraser.

Shadows of birds flying past, birds of prey with enormous wingspans, but he could never see the birds themselves. He squinted up into the sun, and then he tripped and threw out a leg and woke kicking at the bed.

Uh, he said. Uh. He had trouble throwing off the dream, felt he was still crossing that desert. He was in his mother's room, on her bed, cool with sweat and covered in dirt. Uh, he said.

No light at the edges of the curtains. Darkness. And so it was no longer day. He had slept, and for how long? She could have dug her way out by now.

He got up quick, pulled on shoes and shorts and stumbled down the stairs through the kitchen to the back lawn. Moonlight, the shed lit up in relief, a dark hulk outlined in white, the bone trunks of the orchard arrayed behind. The sky enormous above. He listened but heard only the ringing of his own blood and breath and realized he still had the earplugs in. So he yanked them out and ran closer to the shed, heard wood hitting wood.

He was panicked, couldn't focus on where the sound was coming from, but he saw a plank sticking out, a long slat protruding several feet at the bottom, still attached at the top.

The plank next to it sticking out a few inches, and she was hammering from the inside. The planks wide enough she could slip out if she freed two of them. Very close to making her escape.

No, he said. But she was pounding more quickly now, probably using one of the wooden walnut screens.

He ran around to the toolshed, stumbling through pits he'd made in his shoveling, the earth soft and caving, and when he opened the shed, he couldn't see a thing in there. He needed a hammer, but the tools were a jumble. He felt wooden handles, but everything too big. Damn it, he said.

He ran back around the shed, the dirt itself wanting to slow him down, the entire planet conspiring against him, and he tried to push at the plank she was freeing, tried to push it back in with his hands, but he was too soft. The jolt of her hammering from inside. He kicked at the bottom of the wood, slammed his shoulder, pounded with his fists, but it was hopeless.

He tried the other plank, the one freed except at the very top, and pushed that back in, grabbed the edges of it with his hands, but the nails wouldn't line up with their holes and he couldn't see. And then she mashed his left hand.

Galen screamed. His fingers mangled. His mother yelling a kind of war cry. He held his wounded hand and tried to look at it in the moonlight. The fingers still there, but she'd crushed them with something hard, the corner of a walnut drying rack, and it hurt so much he couldn't breathe. The pain rising like fire.

He tried not to run. He walked fast and carefully into the house, into the bathroom off the kitchen, flicked on the light and could see all the way to white bone on his middle finger. No, he said. He was sobbing, his face wet with tears, and he didn't know what to do. He couldn't call anyone.

He tried to move his fingers, and that made him yell again in pain, but they did move. Nothing severed, but he could see bone and ligament and there was blood and the skin all bunched up to the side and he felt like he was going to faint. He leaned against a wall and looked away from his hand. Don't look, he told himself. Hang on.

She was going to escape. If he didn't get out there and nail those planks down, she was going to escape. He didn't have time to do anything for his hand.

A flashlight, he said. I need a flashlight, and then I need to find a hammer.

He had dumped all the drawers from the kitchen and pantry and entryway, so any flashlight would be out in the pile on the lawn. Shit, he said.

He went out there and it just seemed hopeless. A huge pile of crinkled photos and all the crap underneath. He felt around with his good hand, held his left hand in the air, a horror of pain, blood dripping down his arm. So many shapes in the pile. Things plastic and metal and rubber and paper, and the moonlight no help at all. Kneeling here on the lawn, his mother hammering, about to escape, his hand destroyed, he was doomed. He was going to prison. There was no way out of this. Then he remembered she kept flashlights in the trunk of the car.

He ran to the kitchen, where the keys were hanging, got to the car, opened the trunk, and felt around in her box of emergency supplies. The jug of water, food bars, emergency blanket, and two flashlights. He grabbed one, flicked it on, and ran around the house past the fig tree. The beam jagged, the world revealed in patches.

Dirt in relief, the shed a whirlpool and he was circling it, pulled toward the old wood, sucked toward the center, toward his mother, the earth canting to the side.

He washed up at the toolshed, marooned at its door, darted the beam around and found hammers hanging on a wall, everything arranged. Grabbed one and dropped the flashlight, fought back against the current, the hammer held high like an instrument of war. Aaah, he yelled, slogged along the wall until he could attack the plank she was trying to free.

Galen kicked at the bottom edge with his foot, hunched against the flood and rammed with his shoulder, hammered at the spot where nails met crossbeam. The holes not lined up. Driving the nails in fresh, and that would be stronger anyway. Black wood, old, but it was thick and strong enough still, a hand-sawed plank. Rutted and grooved on the surface.

His mother pounding from the other side and screaming. He could feel the impact. But he kept hammering, drove the two big nails all the way in, then bent down and battered the lower nails that met another crossbeam inches off the ground. He could smell the dirt and realized there was no flood at all. Marooned in a desert. The dirt in motion, though, difficult to keep his footing. All this noise in the middle of the night, but they were alone. No one else in this world.

He drove that plank flat, leaned back and roared into the void, his battle cry, his triumph, and ran into the orchard, wielding his hammer and his mangled hand, terrible appendages both, his claws that could tear at the ceiling of the world and bring it down, the earth cresting beneath him, the furrows moon-painted, and he ran again, leaped from furrow to furrow. The pain a pulse in the pattern, and the rage rose in him and he wanted to kill.

He ran the furrows until he landed full tilt against the plank that was loose, slammed it full body and fell back and rose again to rage against it with his hammer. His mother pushed from the other side, but she was nothing. The nails sinking in, and she could not stop him.

The nails singing higher and higher as they shortened until the blows were flat, the plank was flat, and she had no escape.

You are where you are, he yelled. You are where you fucking are. And then he ran to the pile of old cast-off wood stacked against the hedge. Abandoned wood from ten years ago, from fifty years ago, home of rattlesnake and lizard.

Aaah, he roared at the wood, and he slammed the hammer down, beat at the loose boards to send everything scattering, snake and lizard and spider and anything else. Get the fuck out, he yelled.

The pile a thousand shapes in moonlight, a burrowing of shadow. He pulled a long piece, an old board with nails sticking out, dragged it back to the shed by tucking it under his arm. His left hand maimed and useless, he tried to hold the board against the wall using a knee. He wanted it parallel to the ground, about four feet up, to run across all the vertical planks where they met the crossbeam. He'd make a giant seat belt. To free any plank, his mother would have to free a dozen all together at once. She'd never be able to do it.

He couldn't hold the entire board up, so he tried to get one end at the right level, pinned against the wall with his thigh, and he hammered but the nails poking out the other side were gnarled and ancient and all going different directions. They only scraped and bent and made the board bounce.

Damn it, he said, and let it drop into the dirt. He grabbed the flashlight at the toolshed and walked back to the woodpile. The fury had gone out of him. Just gone suddenly, and he felt so sorry for himself, for his mangled hand. He would need to clean it, and wrap it, and he couldn't imagine even touching that area.

The flashlight flattening the woodpile, showing dusty gray, the nails orange. Not a single clean piece of wood, nothing easy.

Galen flicked off the flashlight, walked toward the trees and lay down in a furrow. Held his left hand on his chest, careful. He didn't know why he felt so lost suddenly. As if there were nothing to live for.

The stars fading, the sky a deep dark blue, the earliest sign of day. The dirt at his back still warm from the last day, the dry dead weeds all around him motionless, and what was coming was a scorcher, a day without breeze, a day in an oven. The air already warm and waiting.

He didn't want to see the sun. He wanted it not to rise today, and he thought he'd be willing to spend the rest of his life in this time of day right here, with the sky a beautiful dark blue and the air warm and the moon going down. A near darkness, everything present but not fully formed, the entire world in a state of becoming but not yet arrived. That would be the best time, the best kind of moment to hold forever. He would like that.

But instead, the very worst was coming, he knew. The sky would wash out and bake and the earth would set on fire with no air to breathe and he'd hammer at misshapen pieces of wood as his mother screamed in her cage. That was what he had waiting for him.

So as the sky began to lighten, as the dark blue became a lighter blue and shifted toward white, he rose and took off his shoes and shorts and stood naked, ready for the immolation, ready to be engulfed in fire, and he stepped over the rough ground to the toolshed.

He searched along small shelves, able to see now, until he found nails, sturdy steel nails four inches long. He grabbed the nails with his good hand and walked over to the wall.

The old board lay on the ground with its twisted nails reaching upward, and he understood now that the other side was flat. He'd been on a fool's errand before. He set his hammer and nails close along the wall, then lifted an end of the board, set its flat face against the shed, and reached down for a nail.

He'd have to hold the nail in place with his left hand. There was no other way. He tried to use only his thumb and pinkie, and he tapped the nail very carefully with the hammer. If he missed, the pain would be unbelievable.

He could hear his mother crying. He needed the earplugs again. But he tapped at the nail, then let go and swung carefully, measured blows, drove in the first nail.

You're not getting out, he said. I'm nailing a band around the entire shed, all the planks linked.

I'm your mother.

You're the one making me do this. And that's fine. You're the last attachment, and so it makes sense that everything should feel like hell.

I'm your mother.

Galen lifted the other end of the board and made sure it was lined up with the crossbeam behind the planks. He had to nail into that beam.

People are real, Galen.

He held another nail with his thumb and pinkie, tapped lightly. That sound of metal on metal, the sound of what people were, makers of metal. He could be making coins, minting right here at the shed. Stamping his own image, and why not? The world was only what each of us made of it. His coin would be known as The

Galen. A perfect task for becoming. Coins were just like that dark blue sky, the day about to be.

Lightening quickly now, though, the heavens washing out, everything taken away too soon, all comfort, a test. He would be tested today, he knew.

He walked back to the woodpile for the next piece. No need to choose, because he'd have to use them all. A two-by-two this time, very long and light and perfect for the task. He dragged it into place, held one end up against the planks, set his nail and tapped. No stamp for the design of his face, but each coin individually tapped, each one a sculpture, civilization slowed down. A final recognition that the hordes did not exist. There was no one to make coins for. Beyond this shed and this dirt and the hedge leading down the lane, beyond the orchard and the high wall, there was no one. Galen let his breath slow, a long exhale. There was no one. He could relax, let the attachment go. The pain in his hand, also, an illusion. If he focused on his exhale, the pain paled. It receded and curled away like the snake it was.

I need water, she said, her voice a rough breath. He could hear now how dry it was. But he needed to focus on this new meditation, the hammering.

Each nail individual, metal worked by machine but not perfect, not without variation in how the tip had been sheared or the head formed. Lines cut on the shaft, also, and in this light, there was no shadow. Light as a presence, without source or direction or heat, a cold illumination that was general, and it was only in this light that you could see the true shape of a thing, the fullness of a nail. The robust presence of a nail. It might as well have been sixty feet high. Peering at it up close, it became enormous. A shape-shifter.

Galen held the nail with thumb and pinkie. His blood no longer dripping, clotted now, beginning to scab, and it looked a dark iron red in this light. The skin that had been bunched and torn seemed no longer a part of him. It would dry and fade and fall away. What was exposed now would be covered, and soon it would seem almost that this had never happened.

t was tempting to think of those first shafts of light as fingers as they reached into the leaves of walnuts. But this was a second rising. That was important to remember. The first, the light, the illumination, was a gift. The second, the actual presence, was something else. The second rising was samsara. When we grew old enough for sex, that was our second birth, and that birth was a deformation, a reshaping from the clay of the first birth, and who we became then was something we had to run from for the rest of our lives.

Galen pressed back against the shed wall, stood with his arms out and his eyes closed and waited for the moment he would be blasted by the sun. Nailed to the cross. We were all sacrificed, every day, and no one could do it for us. That was the truth.

Water, his mother said.

Shh, he said. I'm focusing.

I'm going to die. If you don't let me out, if I don't have water, I'll die.

Shh, he said.

Your mother is going to die. Your own mother.

Galen tried to focus only on the sun. He could feel its presence higher on the shed wall, could feel the radiation of that sudden heat. In moments, it would tick downward and set him on fire.

You were named after a doctor, Galen. An ancient Greek physician. You were supposed to help people. You were supposed to be different.

He thought of the earplugs. They were over on the lawn, or he could look for new ones. But he didn't think he'd make it back in time for that first sun. It was rising quickly, but we should call it lowering, the rays of light levered down onto us, a giant seesaw balanced at the edge of the globe. He could feel the wood burning above him. So he held on, tried to just ignore her.

Galen.

His shoulders getting sore from holding his arms out. He didn't feel he could hold them up much longer. Come on, he said. Come on. He wanted to feel his sacrifice. He wanted to feel the shape of the cross as the sun hit.

I won't report you.

Shh, he said. He felt it, finally, in his hair, across his forehead, the heat, the burn, but not as hot as he had imagined. The power he had imagined was not there. He would not be set on fire, only warmed a bit, disappointing as always. The sun a cataclysm, billions of atomic bombs going off every moment, but it was too far away, just like everything else. Everything he wanted to reach was always just outside of his grasp. The world a small emptiness, like looking through the wrong end of a telescope.

Galen let his arms fall, his shoulders burning hotter than the sun, stupidly. The sun moving down over his face and neck and onto his bare chest.

I won't report you to the police. I won't say anything. And you don't have to move out. We'll just go back to the way things were.

Yeah right, Galen said. The minute you're out, the cops will pull up, and they'll chase me down and put me in chains or whatever it is you said.

I'll sign something. We can write something.

My fingerprints are on the lock, just like you said. And you'll show them you haven't had any water. You'll say I made you sign. You've made it all impossible.

The sun moving down his chest, and the air already warmer. Not the sudden fire he wanted but instead a gradual cooking in an oven. He was going to be baked, and there was nothing glorious or interesting about that.

We can figure out a way, his mother said. We just have to work together.

The work I have to do is nailing these boards, he said. So you can't pull your little stunt again. And I have to do it before the day gets too hot.

Galen, she said, but he walked away into the orchard, lay down in the dirt and rolled in it, used his good hand to cover himself completely with dirt, rubbed it into his skin, into his hair, gave himself a coating against the sun. He would not wear clothing again. That was his decision. He would wear only dirt, because dirt was his meditation, and he needed to not ever forget about dirt.

Good smell of dirt, and of weeds. He crawled along the ground, careful not to put any weight on his damaged fingers, using his palm instead, and smelled, and there was one smell stronger than all others, pungent, not a sweet smell, and he found it, finally, along the edge of an irrigated row near a walnut trunk, a place of more water and shade. A pale green that was bluish, almost, and a velvety sheen to the leaves. A plant he had never noticed before, and he didn't know its name. It seemed so unlikely here, made possible only by the irrigation. A plant almost flat, its leaves reaching out along the ground like the legs of a starfish. A roamer, come from another world. The orchard suddenly new, a place he had never seen before.

This was the key, finding the new world within the old. The bitter stinky plant a perfect reminder. Somehow he had never noticed this powerful smell, never seen this unlikely, lush and velvety plant in the midst of all the dry weeds. And this was exactly what he needed to find in the dry husks of all the illusions of self. Something more pungent than self, something more unlikely and from farther away.

Galen lay beside the plant because he knew the irrigation system would turn on soon, and he wanted to be here when the water released. He wanted to feel this plant reaching for the water. Brother plant, he said. Almost time to drink. And he realized he was so incredibly thirsty himself. And starving. But that could be ignored. That was only the body.

He was very tired, so he closed his eyes. The smell of this plant a strong medicine, overpowering, and he stretched and traveled in that smell, elongated like the furrows, and he dreamed nothing he would remember, was lost in blackness and forgetting and the void we all return to, surfaced and was lost and surfaced again and finally he heard the water.

The air hot now. The water trickling in the furrows. He knew he should feel panic, should check to see his mother hadn't escaped, but he didn't feel any panic at all. He leaned closer to the irrigation tubing and put his lips to it, sucked in cool water. Amazing, water. Feeling it on his lips, in his mouth, was a kind of peace. A relaxing of the body, a relaxing of need, of desperation. This was what his mother needed. Something so simple, so basic, and how long could we go without it? Galen didn't know, but it couldn't be long. We needed air more desperately. We couldn't do without that for more than two or three minutes, but water was next. Water was not a luxury.

He should want to bring water to his mother. That should be as basic a need in him as this need to drink or the need to breathe. And yet it was missing. He felt nothing. And that was worth exploring. How could he feel nothing?

Galen sucked at the tubing, suckled at a kind of tit, closing his eyes and humming as he felt the water. Philosophy was meant to do this. Philosophy was meant to make it possible to not bring your own mother a drink of water as she was dying of thirst. And religion was meant to make you believe that what you'd done or not done was good, and right, so it was even more powerful. But what Galen was feeling, or not feeling, was something beyond philosophy or religion, because those were still systems of attachment. What he was feeling was peace, simply peace, and that was the effect of detachment. You could never feel or see detachment itself but only its sign, this flood of peace. Or maybe flood was too active a thought. The important thing was the knowledge, or awareness, that there was no such thing as his mother to be attached to. Then there was no one to bring water to. This was truth.

Galen rose and felt ready to complete the task of nailing the boards. He looked at his injured hand, dirty and dark now, red-brown, and he thought maybe he'd never clean it. He'd let it just be whatever it was going to be. It still hurt, but not as sharply as before. It felt stiff.

He strode over to the pile for a new piece of wood, the sun pressing down, and was squinting so much in the glare his eyes were hardly open. The ground burning his feet. The feet were a problem. He didn't know how he'd get through the day with bare feet. He tried to just ignore the pain, tried to make his feet not a part of him.

He was dizzy, too, from lack of food, but he liked this dizziness. He could use it to get past everything else. He dragged a six-foot board over to the shed wall and aligned it, tapped a nail carefully, drove it in and raised the other end, tapped and drove another nail.

I have a new plan, his mother said.

I don't want to hear your plan.

This is a good one. You'll like this one. Her voice was only a whisper from somewhere in the darkness of the shed.

Galen needed to drive a nail into every vertical plank, so that they were all connected. Each horizontal board a seat belt with a dozen nails. It would take some time.

I have a different checkbook, she said. One as executor of the trust.

I'm not interested.

It doesn't have any limit for amount.

Please shut up.

Galen, you could have a million dollars, more than a million. You could withdraw it all, or maybe leave me just a little bit, and then you could go away, and when you're safely away, you could call the police or fire department and have them come rescue me.

Galen tried to focus on the hammering. The sun merciless, a fire on his back, and his feet damaged. Damn it, he said. I can't focus. Why the fuck didn't we use some of that money? I can't believe you.

I didn't want you to go.

What?

I didn't want you to leave me. I didn't want you to go to college. That was all. I wasn't trying to keep the money to myself. I just didn't want to lose you, Galen.

You're sick.

I love you, Galen.

You're crazy. Stop talking to me.

I only wanted the best for you, Galen. I've always loved you.

Shut up.

And you can take everything now. You can have whatever life you want.

Galen hated all of this. And his feet were burning. He couldn't just stand here. So he hopped around to the shaded side. Ow, he said, and he sat in the dirt and touched one foot with his good hand and could feel how hot and tender the skin had become.

You'll have so much money you can do whatever you want, she whispered. She had followed him to this side. You'll never have to work. You can buy a house somewhere.

Shut up! he screamed. His throat blown out, head dizzy, lost again. She had kept him from living his life. She had done the same to Helen and Jennifer. She had lied to everyone for years. He wanted to take the hammer to her head.

You could go to Mexico.

Damn it! he yelled. Shut the fuck up! You're trying to destroy me.

I'm trying to live. I'm trying to not die in here.

Galen struggled to recover that sense of peace he had felt lying next to the irrigation, drinking the water. How could that leave so quickly? He was like a Ping-Pong ball, bouncing back and forth.

He needed shoes. He wasn't going to be able to focus and get the boards done without shoes. So he hopped into the orchard, trying to keep his feet from touching the burning dirt, and found his shoes in a furrow alongside his shorts. He sat and tied the shoes as quickly as possible, the tender skin of his butt burning.

Okay, he said, standing up. I'm ready. No more distraction. The bottoms of his feet still hurt inside the shoes. The soles really had burned, damaged. It was amazing to him that humans had survived at all. We needed tougher feet, and more hair, or even hard shells, some sort of covering.

He dragged another board, squinting in the glare, and raised and hammered it against the shed as the sun roasted his back. The sweat appearing almost instantly everywhere, the air a coffin, close and thick and unbreathable. He pulled another piece of wood, and another, and found a nice rhythm, finally. The nails hot in his fingers, his mangled hand alive in pain.

He was so dizzy with hunger, he didn't try to find the meditation. He tried only to hang on and remain upright. Just lifting each board and setting the nail and tapping in carefully, then driving. Whenever the burning on his back and shoulders and neck seemed desperate, he reached into the fresh dirt loose from his shoveling and covered himself with it, the sweat making a kind of mud paste that would protect him.

His mother destroying him and claiming to love him, same as Helen with Jennifer. Though Helen actually fought for Jennifer. He could believe Helen. She seemed possible. His mother did not seem possible.

Galen made good progress. The sun high overhead, no shadows or shade anywhere, his eyes burned, the world gone white, and finally he walked around to the spigot near the fig tree and opened it wide, drank deeply in desperate gulps, the water hot at first but then cool, and he knelt down in front of the blast, dipped and rolled in the grass before it and let it cool and clean him, this aerated stream the color of glass, the color of light itself, with the power to stop the burning. He was alert again, revived, and he lay there only a few feet from the shed on his belly with the water cascading on his back and his hand stinging, thinking of his mother who could not reach the water. All this water so close to her. He let it run and run, closed his eyes and thought about just taking a nap, right here, under the water, but he was fully in the sun, and he knew he was burning far worse now, even though he couldn't feel it.

So he rose to his feet, turned off the spigot, and walked back to the closest furrows, the loose dirt, to lift great handfuls over his head and shower in the dirt while he was still wet, while it all would stick and cover and protect.

Water, he heard his mother whisper. She was close to him, only a few feet away behind the wall. Looking at him from between the slats, probably, but he couldn't see her.

No water, he said. No water. Do you think Helen really beats Jennifer? Do you think she actually punches her or kicks her or anything?

She would never do that.

Never mind. I forgot who I was talking with, the denier of all. Nothing ever happened.

My sister would never beat her daughter.

Yeah yeah, he said. Your voice sounds a little dry. He tromped away, around to the other side for his hammer and a new board. He would finish this task. He was so hungry he felt folded in half, even his ribs and spine aching for it, but food could be put off for a long time. He knew that from experience. His own form of denial. Food wasn't necessary at all. He could go weeks without it if he wanted. Only the first couple days were hard. The hunger was not real. It was a false sign.

Galen didn't know why he had first stopped eating. He didn't understand how it had begun. A decision whether or not to drink orange juice. It may have begun there. But who could say the beginning of anything, because it all had started earlier, in previous lives. Not eating was a way of punching through this existence.

The piano, his mother whispered from behind the wall.

Galen pinned a new board and tapped in a nail.

The piano, she whispered again.

He hammered the nail hard, bent it, swore, and placed another, tapped it carefully. His bad hand felt twice as large as a normal hand. Almost impossible to use it to grip something as small as a nail. This was one of the difficult things about a physical existence. The body kept growing and shrinking, always outrageous, and there was no controlling it.

The piano, she whispered.

What? This is so damn annoying. What about the piano?

The checkbook is in the piano.

What the hell? Who were you hiding it from? I didn't even know it existed.

Bring it now. I won't be able to speak soon. I need to sign now.

No. I'm busy. He hammered and kept placing nails. Roasting and sweating and pain everywhere, in his hand, in his gut, the bottoms of his feet, the skin on his back and neck, the dizziness in his head. Everything about this existence related to pain. He was sick of it.

Galen dropped his hammer in the dirt and walked away, across the lawn and into the house. He had been thinking he might never come in here again, had been thinking perhaps he'd just live in the orchard, but here he was already. No resolution lasted.

The inside of the house too comforting, cool and dark and speaking of sleep. He was very tired. He wanted to lie down and forget everything. That was the power of the house, that was how it was dangerous. The house had to be resisted.

He walked to the piano and stood there waiting for his eyes to adjust. The edges floating and shifting, the outline of the wood going white when he blinked. Only a dark shape in shadow, but gradually he could begin to see color, the deep reds and grains in the dark wood, and the piano took up its place, stopped shifting and swimming.

His grandmother playing this piano. Why did he have no memory of that? If they had really sung songs together as a family, if she had played this piano, then why did she stop? Why did everything about that life end before he had memory? If he was supposed to connect to that time, then why had the connection been withheld?

He lifted the top of the piano, a large flat polished piece of wood on a hinge, and he somehow knew to raise the piece of wood inside as a stand. He didn't know how he knew that, some physical imprint without a corollary memory. Perhaps most our memories were like that, no longer accessible but still there somehow, and perhaps that was how we felt our previous lives, also. Their shadows, and their instruction, but no longer anything we could see. They waited and gathered and exerted their presence in some other way, so that every choice we made had already been made, and each random action guided, and the self was not an illusory thing at all, but something that could never die.

The checkbook so small, so simple. The idea that it held more than a million dollars seemed impossible. He had wanted a Walkman for years. A Walkman cost about sixty dollars. He had wanted to go to college, and that might have cost ten thousand dollars per year. He had wanted to have a year abroad, and he didn't know what that would have cost, but not much more than a year of college, probably. Everything had been possible, right here, but his mother had said no.

He didn't understand anything about his mother, not one thing. Wanting to keep him here like some replacement husband. He had no idea who she was or how she could make any sense.

He walked out to the lawn to grab a pen from the pile of crap. He needed to burn all of this today. All his tasks piling up. He still had to finish nailing the boards, also, and finish the furrow of dirt the rest of the way around the shed, and it was already afternoon.

He sat under the fig tree, in its good shade, sat at the iron table and looked at the checks.

You have the checkbook, his mother rasped.

Yeah.

Let me sign.

Okay. He knelt at the wall and slipped the checkbook under the wood, in the gap between earth and shed, then slipped the pen under.

I'll leave the amount blank. You can fill in whatever you want.

Sign all of them. But fill some of them out completely. Start with a check for $4,300.

Why $4,300?

Because that's an easy amount. It's nothing.

Okay.

And then let's go for $47,500. Galen wanted to climb into the fig tree to wait, but he couldn't with his bad hand, so he sat in a cast-iron chair at the table and looked at the part of the property he never visited. Behind the house and lawn was a jungle of other trees and bushes, a piece never claimed for the orchard.

Why doesn't the orchard extend all the way? he asked.

What?

The mess on the other side of the lawn. It's a big piece of the property, and nothing was done with it. No walnut trees. Why not?

That was Mom's piece. She was supposed to get a garden, but there was never time.

How come I never heard about that?

I can't speak. I really can't. I need water.

No water.

Then you don't get the checks.

Fine. I don't give a shit. I need to get back to work on the boards anyway. He walked around the shed to the hottest side, near the toolshed, exposed to the full afternoon sun. He wanted the full heat, wanted to get as dizzy as possible. Dragged a splintery board that had been ripped and banged up and removed from something, and held it against the wall.

He tapped a nail and hammered and heard his mother screech, a raw voice he hadn't heard before, a final screech, the end of a voice. It sounded like her throat ripping. And he was fine with that. He didn't fucking care. I didn't hear you, he yelled. What was that you were saying?

No answer, of course. He hammered at the hot nails and decided he didn't need one going into every vertical plank. That was too many. They'd be held in by the seat belt without each needing their own nail.

He dragged another misbegotten piece from the pile, and another, the work becoming a routine, and gradually the glare from the bleached earth was reduced. Shadows forming in the clods and lengthening, and he was belting a new side of the shed, along the sliding bay door, the sun angling to his left, the time passing, a mercy.

The sun itself felt like a witness, always watching. He could see why the Aztecs or Mayans or whatever worshipped the sun. After it baked and burned you all day, the falling could seem like a gift. You could worship what had almost destroyed you. And if you were alone, the sun might even be a companion, moving along steadily, always there.

Galen heard a sound that he hadn't heard in years. He recognized it immediately. The hand crank on the tractor. His mother turning the crank, trying to start the engine.

No, he said. He stood there with the hammer and didn't know what to do. He couldn't get inside, and if he couldn't get inside, he couldn't stop her. She'd start the tractor and come crashing through the wall. The tractor was easily strong enough for that.

Stop, he said. She was slow on the crank, but she might get it to turn over anyway. He was up against the sliding door now, pressed against it, trying to peer in through a crack, but the gaps weren't big enough, and it was too dark in there, too bright out here.

He ran around to the toolshed and tossed all the tools into the dirt: shovels and picks and rakes, clippers, hoes. He needed to clear a space along the wall next to the tractor. He'd be able to see in from there. The crank turning, and she was going faster now.

Wait, he said. Let's talk about this.

No answer. He pressed against the wood, put his hands up to either side to block the light, and he could just see the larger shadow of the tractor, shifting around in his vision. But he still couldn't do anything to keep her from cranking. She would come tearing through the wall into the orchard, and there was a high gear that could go fast, a gear for driving on the road.

Galen left the wall and looked at all the tools he had tossed into the dirt. He needed something like a spear. Something he could throw. That would be his only chance. The pitchfork. That would do it. It wasn't a large one, four spikes six inches long and with a spread of six inches total. He hefted that in his good hand, got the balance, and hurled it toward the walnut trees. It went about thirty feet, falling short of what he'd imagined, but it flew straight, so maybe that was good enough.

But what was he thinking here? That he'd spear his own mother with a pitchfork? That wasn't possible. That was not something he could do.

Galen stood in the sun and closed his eyes and tried to find some guidance. Prison was all he could think of. Dragged away and locked in a cell, and he'd never see the day again. Never see trees, never see dirt, never watch the moon. Never run freely. Never see Jennifer, never go to Europe, never lie down in a furrow and sleep. Never see the mountains again, or the cabin, never listen to Kitaro or read *Siddhartha*. He would be put in a box and the box sealed and placed on a shelf somewhere to wait. And he might simply be forgotten.

Galen spread his arms wide and tried to follow his higher self. He tried to let his crown chakra open.

He could hear the cranking, turning over and over, and she was working hard, turning as fast as possible, but the engine wasn't firing. He didn't know why that was. It maybe just needed to warm up, though that was difficult to believe on a day as hot as this. It was well over a hundred degrees.

The most frightening thought was that the prison might be a psychiatric ward, a crazy farm. That was what she had threatened, and for keeping his mother locked in a shed, they might put him there. Far worse than being put in a box alone, to be put in a box with the insane. And the drugs. They'd pump him so full of drugs he wouldn't know his own mind. Once they had him there, they could do anything they wanted, and no one in the outside world would ever know or care.

Galen shook his head and his hands and all the way down his spine, the heebie-jeebies. He would not go to the nut farm. He was not willing to go there.

He walked over to the pitchfork and picked it up. If she came through that wall, he was ready.

He stood at the corner, where he could cover two walls, and he listened to the cranking. She had to be exhausted. The cranking was tough, and she'd been doing it for some time now. She was slowing a bit.

The sun still hot on his back and neck and butt and legs. And what would someone see if they came through the hedge into the orchard? Galen doubted he could make sense to anyone. He was naked except for his shoes, burned and covered in dirt, holding a pitchfork like a spear, waiting, a guardian. Rough boards nailed around the shed in an uneven band, a furrow dug against it. All of this would look crazy, he realized. If you hadn't been here, if you hadn't seen each step happen, then none of it could make any sense.

For the rest of this incarnation, Galen needed to be alone. He could see that now. Other people were the problem. They were distractions and attachments. They were noise. He needed quiet. He needed to hear back across lifetimes, and that required a stillness that was not possible if any other person was near. The final incarnation was meant to be spent in a cave, and this orchard was his cave, protected from the outside world. No one knew to look here. He would be safe here, once he eliminated this final attachment in the form of his mother. He was having to hammer and dig and fight this final battle because it was the inner battle made physical in the outside world. That was the gift he was being given, an external way to stage and complete the inner journey, the final journey before repose. He was creating a fortress against all that would distract. Once she was gone, he would sit in the dirt and listen back across all the shifting forms of self and being, and though he didn't know what was to come after, because he hadn't been there yet, he knew this was what everything was leaning toward.

His mother cranked the tractor for a longer time than he could have imagined. And so he knew this was her final act. She was not saving anything. There would be no attempt to dig her way out or to hammer the planks loose again. If she failed to start the tractor, that would be it. She'd have nothing left.

Galen listened carefully to the cranking, because he knew this was a meditation, a gift she was giving him on her way out. A strange sound and a powerful one because it connected all the way back through his childhood and through her own. It was a sound to begin his journey across lifetimes, a cable he could reach onto that was being winched back into the darkness.

Thank you, he said. I honor this.

With his pitchfork and his covering of dirt, he was being armed for a symbolic journey, and she was the opening.

The sound fainter on each upswing, then hard as she came down, and there was a cough to that sound, the compression in the engine. Galen stepped forward on the cough, stepped into a furrow with his left foot. Then he rocked back on the upswing and stepped forward again as she swung down. A dance.

Galen squatted lower, stepped harder and harder, held the spear high in his right hand. He stamped forward on that beat, shook his spear, felt the heat rise in him, his entire body wet with sweat. He had to find the right sound, the right voice, to go with the stamp, and he was afraid to try, afraid he'd have the wrong sound and wreck the moment. He was building to something here. This was his mother's final gift to him. He didn't know whether to go with a grunt or more of a *ho*. The *ho* more ceremonial, but the grunt more authentic. Or an *aah* that would be more of a yell. He tried to just let whatever would happen happen.

And what came out was a grunt, a low *huh* kind of grunt. And that felt good. That felt right. It was real, just a low grunt, the first sound made by any human, the early sound. He shook his spear and grunted from deep in his gut, deep in his root chakra, his base, his chi.

The grunt shaking all the spirit walls inside him, the long throat chord linking his voice to his chi, even his lung walls shaking, and the good smell of dirt, his guide, with him now, with him always, the dirt, and he reached down with his bad hand, scooped the dirt and threw it into his mouth, howled from the pain, the mangled hand coming alive, and he howled and grunted and chewed the earth and the pain rose in his head in wavy bands, his hand a pulsating mass, so he held that out front, held that to guide him into the spirit world.

We could never see it, but we journeyed through it every moment of every day. The trick was to wake up in the middle of the dream and yet still dream, and then we could battle. To wake up, we had to tear away at illusion, and his hand was good for that. The cranking of the tractor was good for that.

The crank, the *whump* as it went round and round, the cough and compression, his mother a kind of shaman, leading him forward, and he danced, he stamped as hard as he could, he shook everywhere inside, and he tried to dance through time. That was one way to break through the dream, to make time shift, to dance in an older orchard. Old wall, old dirt, dancing back.

The spear an ancient weapon, from the first dance. The long jointed arm a thrower, formed for this. The first man shaking his spear, raging at the wilderness, at the void, claiming the world. Galen tried to dance back in time, tried to reconnect. Tried to make himself that first man, stamping at the earth, fueled by breath, a fire all around him, and he crushed hard enough to break furrow and crust, felt the spear's power, and then he lunged. He lunged into the wall, lunged through the air headfirst with a scream and drove that spear into the wall, into the spirit fortress, and it hit hard and bounced and he flew and banged into the wall with his shoulder and head and fell to the ground and rose again. Aaaah! he yelled. Aaah! His hand a living thing, a hive of pain.

He grabbed his spear and stepped back into place to stamp again. The same piece of earth, his blow felt all through the crust, reaching downward, sending shock waves. He built again, step and rock and the low grunts, feeling his source, the energy coming from deep within him. He would use everything to break through the spirit wall. He would circle back and come from another time.

Galen turned in a circle as he rocked and shook his spear. The shadows long, walnut trees like sentinels, casting their truer selves across furrows. They had been waiting for this, waiting through lifetimes, waiting for him, for his coming. They would rise up out of their shadows in the earth, and that would be their shape. Not the shape of a tree, of what we imagined, but a deeper form. Galen screamed and shook his spear, triumphant. He had seen into the spirit world. This was his first true seeing, to see the trees would form up out of their shadows, that they were made of earth, not of wood. He might even be the first man to have seen this, the first to know the trees. Ho! he yelled, acknowledging the gift. He circled and crushed and looked sideways at the dark long shadows all around him, and he understood now that the stamping of his feet was what would free the spirit selves of the trees. He was the unlocker, the one to break through. He plunged his spear into the earth, rocked the handle as he danced to loosen all that would hold them back.

They were growing as the light fell, and they would rise impossibly tall, great dark earth presences reaching into the sky. They would stride miles at every step, cross continents. They would carry him, loft him, and fling him.

Half waking, Galen lived in the double world, seeing the presences and also still chained to appearances. He had to not look too long at any shadow, because if he did, it became only shadow, and the dirt became only dirt. He had to keep his vision moving, had to keep circling and spinning. Engulfed in fire, unable to breathe, his body failing but spirit gathering.

Galen realized he was singing, a low, guttural song, a song of becoming. Gathering his previous lives around him, he saw that they were time itself. He was summoning time and being in his final burst of becoming.

Galen began to feel afraid of what was happening here. The shamanic was different from the meditative. Shoveling dirt, he had focused on the fling and fall and the nothing. It was a dissipation. But this was a gathering now, something entirely different, something frightening because it might be exactly the wrong path, a trick. How could becoming be the goal? Detachment was supposed to be the goal, and detachment was not the same as becoming.

Galen spun and stamped but he was exhausted and confused. He didn't understand how it all fit together, and his confusion had made the spirit world recede. He was hot and tired and wet and muddy and the shadows of the trees were only shadows, and all had fallen so quickly and so terribly. He could feel the bones in his thin legs, the muscles locked and stiff. Empty, all his movements now.

Galen stopped dancing, stood in place dizzy and hungry and thirsty. He was alone. The air still, no wind. The endless hum of the air conditioners all along the high wall. He realized there was no cranking. That sound had stopped. He wondered how long ago. He had been dancing for a long time.

He dropped the pitchfork. The sun no longer burning, much of the orchard in shadow, and he lay down in a furrow, in the radiating earth, decided he would just lie here until he understood, but he was starving and parched and couldn't focus at all. His head and shoulder hurt from lunging into the shed. So he rose on cramped legs and walked slowly to the house.

That pile on the lawn still waiting to be burned. The grass still waiting to be cut. The house always waiting, through lifetimes. Impossibly large and ornate and white. A solidity that was untrue. The great chimney at the center, and the giant trees. A house that promised peace and reasonable people but had held only crazies. A house that was a way to hide.

Galen walked into the kitchen and went for a glass of water, gulped it down, and then gulped another. And still he felt thirsty.

He didn't know what to eat. Always a problem. He held the refrigerator open and stared blankly at too many items that made no sense. Pickle relish. Not easy to make a meal out of pickle relish. Sauerkraut. He could maybe eat that. In a dish covered with Saran Wrap. He brought it to the kitchen table, took a fork from a drawer. Real silver, unpolished.

It seemed that sauerkraut should go with something. He looked in the pantry, in the canned goods, and found French-cut string beans, took them to the counter, the electric can opener.

He sat and forked the green beans from the can, cold and salty

and without other taste. He chewed and swallowed and it felt like
the inside of his stomach had collapsed and the food was having to
push the folds back open. He forked sauerkraut and liked the vinegar. Vinegar was right.

The house dimmed as he ate. The sky outside turning a darker
blue. He finished the green beans and most of the sauerkraut, then
drank another glass of water and went to the sink, where his mother
usually stood, looked out at the shed and orchard and sky. Everything farther away as the light dimmed, all distance increased.

He thought he might stay at the sink for a while, but found
himself rising up the stairs to his mother's bedroom, stood in the
doorway and swayed in place, thinking nothing, then went to her
bed. The house not hot like outside, the high ceilings and drapes a
sanctuary.

He lay on her bed and closed his eyes and could feel the inside
of him spinning and tilting, everything caving. The dirt on his skin
his blanket, his hand throbbing in a dull and reassuring way, and all
was so peaceful. His mother resting now, too, in that place of her
memories, in her own sanctuary. The land all around them breathing easily, the orchard at rest, the hedges, the fig tree, the oak. All
resting, finally, and the heat fading away. She had wanted to keep
him here, and here he was.

B lack rock. Volcanic. Rock that had boiled, shot through with air. Broken now, severed and sheared and sharp as glass. Pores and hollows. The walnut trees growing from the rock, roots worked into vents and cauldrons, snaking along fissures. Soft flesh of wood encased.

From the surface, no way of telling how far they reached. The roots and trunks white against the black.

Miles between every tree, the orchard grown. And Galen carrying a small sack of water, a sack made of flesh, and he had to let a few drops fall on the roots of each tree. Rare that he saw a tree at all. Mostly wandering, looking for the next, and the land growing as he walked, cracking and stretching, opening great chasms that filled with melt and hardened and he continued on.

His feet torn, unshod, and clicking on the rock. His joints clicking also, each movement of knee or hip or ankle, even the movement of his eyes. The sack thick with fat held very little water, and it had to be held carefully. He must not drop it. If he dropped it, all would be lost. And so he stared at the rock, careful in placing each step and click.

Galen knew that years were passing, that he had no hope of reaching every tree in time. He might not reach even the next tree.

The water disappearing as he walked, becoming only a sheen on the walls of fat.

The surface of the planet was bending. But the other problem was the melt. The melt delayed him, because he couldn't help gazing. A deep red, rock transformed, all patterns round and edged with black, a slow boil and upwelling, and then the fade as the rock cooled and lost its color.

He continued walking even as he woke, held on to the dream, tried to extend and understand. Walking toward the next tree. Strange dream. He tried not to think, tried not to let his waking mind take over, tried to fall back again into the larger mind. But the small mind refused. Galen had to pee, and the small mind was very focused on that.

Fine, he said, and he rose and peed in his mother's toilet and nothing felt real. Standing here in his mother's bathroom, covered in dirt. Sleeping in his mother's bed. His mother out there still. None of this could make any sense, and he didn't want to participate in it anymore. He wanted to fall back asleep and dream.

So Galen lay down and refused to wake. He felt exhausted still, enormously tired, and was able to fall back out of mind until he woke again this time without dreams and his mouth dry and stomach demanding food.

He rose and peed again and bent down to drink out of the sink faucet, gulp after gulp, so dry. His mother's toothbrush, purple and white, something from another life, a life already difficult to remember or even believe. Who we are now, he said.

He walked downstairs to the kitchen, legs sore and tight, his joints clicking just like in the dream, bone ends catching as they worked. His hips no longer arranged correctly.

The problem again of what to eat. A constant reminder that incarnation was enslavement. He wanted to just be done with eating, wanted to rip his stomach out and move on to other things. But it would not be ignored. Demanding and desperate, and until he gave it what it wanted, he would have no peace.

What would your highness like? he asked. The pantry a jumble of colors, but the most colorful of all a large can of fruit cocktail. The bright red cherries, yellows and whites and greens, the grapes. All in syrup too sweet.

The can heavy. He held it up to the opener as it circled. Fruit cocktail sandwiches, he said.

Galen heaped the fruit into a hammock of bread and had a bite, the bread gone doughy from the wet. He ate a cherry on its own, could taste the dye. Other than the cherries, all the other fruit had become the same, all one taste. It was simply "fruit," not peach or pear or grape or whatever else. And this was the same for people's lives, going to work at the same jobs, living in the same houses, those houses over the high fence. But not Galen's life. Galen's life was not like theirs. He was wearing dirt, and that was the big difference. You knew a man by how he dressed.

Galen was watering trees today. He would need to carry his sack of flesh with its small bit of water and bring a few drops to each tree across a landscape of black rock and melt. Except that the orchard was dirt, not rock, and there were not miles between each trunk, opening and increasing. How the dream world fit into the waking world was never clear.

Galen gave up on the bread, forked the fruit in great mouthfuls and chewed quickly. He knew that what he was afraid to think of was his mother. Food always a substitute, never itself. He tied his shoes and stepped out into the oven.

Afternoon already, a kiln for baking bricks, dry and stinging his lungs. Each day seemed hotter than any other, but they were all the same inferno. The shed bleached in glare, heat waves in the orchard, actual heat waves like melted glass a few feet from the ground, distorting the shapes of the trunks and weeds and furrows. The orchard looked like it might be only ten feet deep, something you could cross in one long step. Or it could be miles deep. Distance impossible to tell.

He didn't want to go near the shed. Its rough belt of wood, a partial furrow on the orchard wall, his mother somewhere inside. That his life had funneled down to this wasn't fair.

He stepped out of the shade into the full blast of the sun. The stream of light at impossible speed and pulsing as it hit, tearing away all. Any shelter was temporary. In the end, the sun would take everything.

Galen nearly blind as he walked. This body with the landscape shifting around it but the light constant. He could not stay out here long.

Everything shrank in the glare. The roof of the shed maybe a foot or two lower, the boards thinner by half an inch. The fig tree more squat to the ground, not as tall as before. The furrows shallow. Galen didn't know what that meant, that everything grew as the light faded and shrank again in the day. This was true of presence, also, that shadow and night seemed inhabited and the bright day did not. All life was emptied at midday, and yet Galen had to roam around in it for countless hours, always roaming a desert.

The path from lawn into orchard always along the left side, this sunrise wall, east facing. Here was where his mother had hammered the planks loose. Here was where he had stood in the shape of a cross. And here now was where he found the checkbook, pushed out in the gap between human and solid earth, armored by rock, where he had not been able to dig a furrow.

He picked it up and flipped through the pages, squinting. She had signed every check, and a dozen of them had amounts. The last one $430,000. All this money.

He looked away at the walnut trees, whited. Looked again at the checkbook, held it in both hands, turned it over and found a note. *Please, son. I love you.*

And yet she'd been willing to throw him away. She had called him an animal and wanted him to spend the rest of his days in a cage like an animal.

Please, son. I love you. He didn't know what to think of this, because here was the problem: he believed her. He knew that he owed her everything, that every son owes his mother everything. And he knew that she loved him, and that he loved her. But he also knew that she had been willing to throw him away. And it was not possible to get these things to fit together.

Mom? he called.

He could not stand here long. The sun would not allow it. Mom, he repeated.

But there was no answer. He walked up close, put his ear at a gap between boards and tried to hear movement, a dry voice, anything.

The landings of grasshoppers, a yellow sound, without depth. The distant, unstoppable hum of the air conditioners. A car passing on the road, much muffled by the hedges. But nothing else. Only the sound of his own blood and breath.

He walked to the next wall, with the bay door and its old rusty lock. Mom? he tried again, but no answer. So he went to the third wall, the side with the toolshed, where he would bake through the afternoon, and he stood there squinting at old wood. I can't make any sense of you, he said.

She had been excited, breathless and excited at the thought of him being dragged away to prison. She had said she was afraid of him, but why? He had done nothing. She had called him an abuser and a rapist, her own son who had done nothing. What he'd shared with Jennifer was not a crime.

You, he said. You have done this. You have forced me into this.

She was not responding. He wanted to talk with her. He wanted to find out why.

It's not fair, he said, that I get one parent and she's crazy. That's not fair. And here I am talking to a wall, just as crazy as you. Thanks, Mom.

There would be no peace, ever. He could see that. His mind would always be chained to thinking about her. Guilt and anger and shame and everything else that made a life smaller. She had destroyed everything. He had wanted to focus on his meditation. That was all. He had wanted to be left alone.

He couldn't just stand here. He went to the lock, held it in his hand, yanked at it to see whether it might open. He had no idea where the key might be. Rusty old lock, much bigger than needed, thick steel.

Galen looked in the toolshed for the key. Along the small shelves and ledges built into the walls, added to over the years. His grandfather a kind of pack rat. And the problem was not in finding a key. The problem was that there were too many keys, dozens of them, on chains and lying individually in the dust. So he collected them all and brought them back to the bay door, set them carefully in the bottom of a furrow.

Rusty, dirty keys and a rusty, dirty lock. Even if he found the right key, he might not know, because it wouldn't go in easily. The lock so hot in this sun it was burning his hands, but he tried key after key, finally went for cotton gloves from the toolshed, then tried more keys.

I haven't decided anything, he told her. Don't get your hopes up. I'm just seeing if I have the key.

Then he thought of WD-40. That would help tremendously. He walked past all the crap scattered in the dirt, everything he had thrown out of the toolshed, and didn't see a blue and yellow can. He stepped inside the toolshed and let his vision adjust, knelt and searched along the lower wall under a slanting roof and found half-used cans of paint, grease and engine oil, and finally the WD-40.

Galen sprayed the keyhole in the lock, leaned away from the smell, sprayed the pile of keys in the dirt. He needed a rag or something to clean them, but he had only the cotton gloves. So before he tried each key, he wiped it, both sides, on the glove of his left hand, on the palm, the fingers still curled in pain, that hand turning into a club.

A few of the keys were the right size and went partway in, but not one of them went all the way in.

How is this possible? he asked. A million keys and one lock. How could I not have the key here? Where's the key, Mom?

Not one of them fit. He walked around to the lawn, to the pile of crinkled photos and crap from the drawers. He took the glove off his right hand and sifted for keys, found dozens more. It didn't make any sense that there were so many keys, as if his family had owned all the world. What did they all unlock? What was left? All the illusions everywhere in this life, and we were left holding a pile of keys to nothing. This is perfect, Galen said. This is exactly how things are.

He carried them all back to the lock, and he knew none would fit but he tried them anyway, one at a time, in what felt like a ritual, nothing less than sacred. I honor this, he said. If a key fits, you'll go free.

Light-headed from the WD-40 vaporizing. Light-headed from the sun, from living in this incinerator. A grasshopper landed on the lock and he let it stay there and watch. A husk of a body, something that could be threshed like wheat. Good bread of grasshopper, something Galen might try.

When the last key failed, he let the lock fall back against wood and the grasshopper launched. Galen on his knees in the dirt, burning. He didn't know what to do next.

His mother was dying on the other side of this door. There was no point in hiding that. He hadn't made any decision. He had never made a decision to let her die, but she was dying anyway. It was her own fault, something she had done to herself, but he was responsible too. She had made him responsible. Damn you, he said.

Our actions controlled beyond what we could know. Galen could never have seen any of this, and yet this is what he had been given.

He felt like he would die, too, if he remained kneeling here in the dirt and sun, so he rose, his legs stiff, and walked around to the fig tree and the spigot and opened the water wide, drank gulp after gulp. He could try to get some water to her, put the hose through a gap in the wall and let it run. He might have to do that. Or let her out. But he didn't see how he could let her out. She had left him with no options. Thanks a lot, he said.

Galen walked into the wilderness on the other side of the lawn, into what was supposed to be his grandmother's garden. Thistle and dry yellow grass to his shoulders, his feet falling out of sight, rattlesnake and lizard. He didn't care what happened. Live oak, its leaves knit up in spiny points, scratching all along his bare skin, through his shield of dirt. A thicket of them, and he pushed his way through, liked the awareness that came with all the cuts. A forest for flaying. The leaves only half alive, half green, the trunks thin and numerous and hidden in shadow. His head still exposed to the sun as he pushed between them, short trees without real shade.

This wilderness extended, stretched on and on, thistle and grass and live oak. His thighs and stomach caught by the thistles, his feet pierced by thorn and branch and rock. He held his arms out when he could, to catch more thistle and oak. A shallow dry sea he was wading through, merciless sea, his eyes stinging, the taste of salt, and he the only man to wade here.

Manzanita. This was what Galen found in that wilderness. He didn't see it coming, didn't know it could grow here, thought it grew only on hills. And then he was standing before it, red bark thin as paper. Smooth trunks almost iridescent, the shaded sections pooling light into turquoise and the shimmer of eyes. The trunks swollen, obscene red limbs, round and full, bursting the skin where it fell away in scrolls. He reached out to pluck a scroll, left a rip that showed a lighter white-green, the flesh not red.

So little to hold in his hand, this curl. Nothing at all once it was separated from the tree, from its becoming. He dropped it and heard no sound. The leaves bright green and hard, firm teardrops no bigger than an inch across, velvety and improbable in this heat, among everything else so dry.

The manzanita seemed to have its own source of water, hoarded and secret. A dozen trunks all curved outward in a kind of basket, fending off and creating space. Galen imagined a taproot, something that reached farther down than the others would ever know, but he wasn't sure that was true. It might be drifting shallow on the surface.

He wanted to honor the manzanita but didn't know how. All this time, and he hadn't known it was here. He crouched down and crawled in close but couldn't get to the center. A kind of cage to keep him out.

Galen crawled away from the manzanita, liked moving on hand and knee, liked seeing the ground and having the dry grass rise high above him. So much better not to have blank air above. The way his body moved in a crawl, catlike, and his awareness increased. Sound and vision in close, and a sense that other things watched him. He wanted to come face-to-face with a rattlesnake, wanted to feel his heart leap.

He imagined his mother down close to the ground, lying on her side, conserving. Hidden away in the shade of the shed, near the walnut drying racks, seeking cool earth. He imagined her skin thinning like paper, like the manzanita bark, drying.

Thistle in close a kind of fortress rising in layers, broadest at the base. Waxy green and thick, with white milky veins, and the purple flower far above made of tassle, of silk. Thistle and manzanita could hold color as the others dried and went yellow and brown, but thistle the more lush, that white milk pulled from nowhere.

Galen crawled toward the base of a live oak, into greater shade, the spines writing along his back in thin cuts. Fallen leaves cutting his hands and knees. Ants everywhere, red and black, living in deadfall. Galen lay down among them and waited. Lay here as his mother lay there, sharing the same ground.

These are the true things, Galen said. My mother might be dead. Or she's dying. And I'm not helping her. I didn't bring her water, and I'm not helping her now. I'm lying here in dry grass and live oak, and I'm waiting for her to die. That's what I'm really doing.

The ants all over his body, small visitors taking their impossible walks. To the moon and back was nothing for an ant. Whenever an ant returned home, it headed out again. Because an ant never had to think about what it was doing. There were no ants trying to understand their mothers.

I don't understand much, Galen said. I'm working on it, but I still don't understand much. I have a few ideas. I know she was trying to send her father to prison. I know she confused the two of us. I think that's right. And because she hated her father, I think maybe she always hated me. I think maybe it was war from the very start, and either she had to die or I had to die.

He ran his good hand through the fallen live oak leaves, all the tiny spines. The dirt dry underneath. He cleared a patch and could see cracks.

He thought of the fuck-grimace on his face, his mother seeing that, hearing him moan as he came onto Jennifer. The shame he'd felt. That was the problem with mothers. Always watching, and who we became wasn't something we wanted anyone to see. Maybe our mothers had to die. The idea that we wanted to sleep with our mothers and kill our fathers was ridiculous. We could never even find our fathers.

War from the very start. Our mothers needed to kill us too. His grandmother would never be good while Helen was alive. She'd never be able to think of herself as good. Her entire life would have to be constantly forgotten. And Helen would never be able to erase her childhood until she erased Jennifer. Jennifer an unwelcome reminder.

Helen was fighting for Jennifer, trying to save her from the favoritism and lies and money and everything else, but no one had tried to save Helen when she was young, and her rage at this was why she could be abusing Jennifer. Jennifer had said that was how they showed love. So Helen was a kind of tragedy, destroying her daughter as she tried to save her, every step of her life blind, all of her efforts undoing all her other efforts. And Galen's own mother even more blind, keeping a son as a husband to punish a father.

This land was not meant to be lived on. There could be no belonging here. His family had come from Germany and Iceland and settled in the middle of a desert. They had put up the hedge, let developers put up the wall, separated themselves from other people. They found the one country in the world where it was possible to live entirely unconnected to anyone else. The one country where family could be reduced to only family, isolated, and his grandfather formed that family in his own image. A forging in violence and shame that had gained an unstoppable momentum. Helen had a daughter and saw herself in that daughter and punished. Galen's mother had a son and saw her father in that son and punished. Helen and his mother doing essentially the same thing, both out of control.

Galen didn't know how to find another path. He would wait for his mother to die, but he didn't know what would happen after that. He might bring his grandmother home. That seemed right. But beyond that, he couldn't see a thing.

Some of the red ants were biting him, which was annoying, so Galen crawled out from under the live oak and stood in the tall grass. Yellow-brown sea, and he was submerged to the shoulders. He waded farther into nowhere, and he felt a sadness all through him. A tired, heavy sadness. Dry stalks, no wind, the sun pressing down, and the sadness hung from each rib. This was not a meditation, only a weight. His family a weight. Better if none of them had ever been. He walked and burned and was scratched and pierced by unnumbered things as he passed, and this wandering was all that was left him, just wandering in circles until finally he was standing at the edge of the lawn again, looking down at the artificially green grass, the oasis.

The pile on the lawn would have to be cleaned up. And his mother's room. And the boards removed from around the shed, and the furrow. The lock. Someone could come and see. He needed to erase all signs.

Looking down at his own body, the dirt covering his feet and legs and belly, he knew this was what he needed to erase first. If anyone saw him like this, they would wonder.

Galen walked into the house, up to his room, to the shower. Cold at first, shivering immediately, the incredible contrast from the oven. But then the water warmed, and he stood in place and watched rivulets of mud, the deltas forming down his legs, like veins, a patchwork of external veins, our blood outside our bodies, provided by the world. The mud clinging to him, large dark islands, wet black and the rivers between them eating away at the banks, rivers reddish from the burned skin exposed.

All of him stinging. His hand the worst, but all his burned skin, also. He turned up the temperature, wanted to see his flesh glow hot, wanted the rivers to look like embers. The mud persistent, clinging and heavy, baked onto him. Mostly gone from his arms and shoulders and chest, where the water hit, but holding still on his thighs and almost untouched on his shins. Red rivers widening slowly.

Galen didn't know what any of it meant, but he knew dirt was his teacher. At every moment, unexpected, dirt was showing him something. Better than going to a university. He might never go, even with all the money. He might just stay right here, in this old house and orchard, and learn everything.

But it was hard to believe in a future, hard to care.

He was in so much pain he finally had to turn the temperature down. His whole body pulsing in the burn. He fumbled at the shampoo with one hand, tried to work it into his hair but there was so much dirt. The top of his head caked, so he put his head in the stream of water and just ran one hand over it for a long time. This felt right, standing with his head bowed and rubbing a hand over it, an expression of despair. He moaned a little to go with it, and that felt right. Waiting for his mother to die. Transcendence seemed far away. The big problem was that we could never see far enough ahead. How could we transcend if we kept getting ambushed?

Great smears of mud across his thighs as he scrubbed with soap. The black becoming lighter brown and then washed away. Small stones gathered at the drain, and bits of leaf and grass and thorn.

Bending down for his shins and calves, scrubbing until the last of the dirt was gone, a kind of loss. It had felt right to be covered in dirt. He was naked now.

He turned off the water. His hand did not look good. Sore and a bit puffy and red at the edges, infected. He dried carefully with a towel and looked for Neosporin. Neosporin was a belief in the future. He found it in a cabinet and applied liberally, then wrapped his hand in clean gauze, padded into his room and pulled on a clean T-shirt and shorts, clean socks and his dirty old Converse high-tops. Then he went to her room.

Everything on the floor. The bed dark with dirt. He felt tired. He didn't want to deal with this. And the shed was more important anyway. He had to remove the boards he'd nailed around in a kind of belt. That would draw attention.

Half waking, Galen said. We are half waking, going through the motions. I hammered all those nails, and now I need to take them out.

Down the stairs and into the kitchen, where he gulped at water, always so thirsty, and he ate two pieces of bread and then drank more water.

Outside, it was late afternoon now. Time passing. That was what he wanted. He wanted the day to end, but time was so slow.

Shadow hanging off the east wall, stretching into the furrows.

He put his ear to the wall, listened, tried to hear any sign of her, even the lightest breathing, but she had vanished. He didn't know how long it took to die from no water. He didn't want to go in too early and find her alive. Because if he found her alive, he would call an ambulance. It would be impossible not to do that. So he needed to wait.

He walked around to the toolshed, feeling too clean, too unconnected. He was no longer a part of this place. He looked around for a hammer and then realized a crowbar might be faster. His grandfather had three of them leaning in a corner. Old metal, unpainted, wiped in oil, rough at the edges. Galen picked up the slimmest, shortest one, and even that was heavy. Tool users. It was possible to have an entirely different view of humans. No souls, no transcendence, no past lives, only animals that had learned better tricks. Everything pointless.

Galen used his opposable thumbs, gripped the crowbar and slotted its thin face between board and wall. Levered and popped the end of that board free, worked along until it fell to the earth, undone. Moved along to the next board, worked the hungry thin teeth of the crowbar.

The sun on the back of his neck. His body a slick, the T-shirt draping close. He felt dizzy, and that was fine. He tried to lose himself in the work and not think. The furrow along the wall annoying because it kept him from stepping as close as he would have liked. He had to lean in, and his back was cramping up.

Removing the boards was so much faster than nailing them. Galen was on the second side in no time, along the wall with the bay door, his back to the trees. The old lock still hanging there. He didn't know what he would do about that. He still didn't have the key, and it seemed too big to break with a crowbar.

For now he would focus only on removing the boards. One task at a time. They fell off like scabs, rough and uneven, discarded wood, lying in the dirt with their nails sticking up. Galen had the idea of dismantling the entire shed. He could remove one plank at a time and drag them all into the orchard. The shed dispersed, planks lying along every furrow. The tractor and the walnut drying screens in their stacks would be exposed to the sun and moon. He liked that idea. Just undo everything and wait in the orchard until the wood decayed and became earth again and there would be no sign that the shed had ever existed. He would be old by then, and his final project would be to undo the house. He would take it apart board by board, just as he had done to the shed, and in the end, only the piano would remain, and maybe that cool wooden floor, exposed now to the sun.

If only Galen could live long enough to watch boards decay into dust. To stand here in the orchard and watch the high wall and housing developments crumble, and watch the land return to desert, with no water and no sign of civilization, and then watch the rains come and plants grow and wind and storms and water increase until he stood in a jungle with palm fronds and ferns and vines and the air filled with water. Galen wanted that. He wanted no part of human society. He wanted to join geologic time. But first he had to get through this one day, and even that seemed as long as the transformation of desert to jungle.

Galen took a break from the crowbar, grabbed a board in his good hand, and dragged it toward the pile along the hedge. Leaving a thin track in the dirt, the only sign remaining, and he could rake that out. The pile reduced to almost nothing, a few scraps, but it would grow again now. Galen took his time walking back for the next board. He didn't really believe anyone would visit. A year from now, Jennifer would need her first check for college. But before that, no one. Removing the boards was another form of going through the motions, another performance for no audience.

He picked up another, dragged it, and listened to the hollow sound that came through the wood. Something faint in addition to the dragging, something transmitted through the length of the board, always more to hear and see. We could never be awake enough. He flopped the board onto the pile, then bent over with his hands on his knees and felt lost, the inside of him a vacuum. He had to breathe, just focus on his breath, and then he stood up again and walked back for another board.

He dragged the boards one at a time, and the sun was lower. It was very slow, but it was lower. He picked up the crowbar again and pried along the eastern wall in shadow. Concealed from the sun. Hidden from all except perhaps his mother. He wondered whether she could still see and hear him, outlined through the slats against the sky. Easiest along the west wall, where he would leave a shadow, much more difficult to find along this wall. A peaceful way to go, not having water. A light-headedness and quiet that would fade eventually into nothing, a meditation on light and sound and air.

Galen worked on the furrow in darkness, no moon. Felt his way along the walls with the shovel. The air shallow, an ebb time. Sound magnified.

He was using the flat-faced shovel, jamming its squared end down along the boards into the loose dirt he had piled, then pulling toward him. The dirt heavy and invisible and loud. The scuff of the face as he dragged each load a few feet, spreading the soil. Making a bed for a new garden, planting his footsteps.

It could seem at times that his mother wasn't really in there. Or that she could vanish on her own. It could seem there were no other people in the world. And whenever he got this sense, he tried to hold on to it, because he liked being the last person on earth. He found that idea enormously comforting.

Galen liked labor. He liked pulling the dirt away from this wall, clearing and smoothing, and he wished that when he'd finished he could start over and find dirt newly piled where he had begun. What was difficult, always, was the transition, moving on to the next thing and settling in. He liked repetition. This was what religion was made of. Repeating the same words over and over, or prostrations, or sitting and focusing on breath after breath. What terrified us was the void, not knowing what would happen next or what we should do or who we should be. Repetition was a focal point, a shelter.

Galen waited in darkness for the rise of that moon. He drove the shovel down, pulled and walked backward and spread the soil, but all the while he was waiting. And when it did finally come, its face was impossibly large, warped by being too close to the earth. A lesson there, the distortion from proximity. The moon would not know its real shape until it hung on its own.

Engorged now with light, fat on the horizon, heavy. The small man kneeling in prayer, magnified so large Galen could see and feel the space above the man's head, the lofting emptiness between the man and the snake's open mouth. Galen let the shovel fall and held his arms out and gazed at the moon, honoring the fullness knowing it was shrinking in every moment, cooling into its harder shape, more distant, going white as bone, the color leaching. Brother moon, he said. Each of us alone on our path.

Galen lowered his arms and looked at the orchard transformed, the trees emerged into the second day, moon's day. The walnuts responsible. Standing here all these years, they'd had some influence over the shape of things. They couldn't deny that.

Galen picked up the shovel and returned to his labor. Finishing the orchard-facing wall, southern wall. The shed placed perfectly to meet the four directions, and that couldn't have been accidental, but Galen didn't know what sense to make of it. Their house to the north, the fig tree and afternoon tea to the north, and the lawn and the large oak with its love seat beneath. All civilization. So perhaps that meant something. The road to the west. The orchard waiting to the south and extending to the east, and Galen realized only now that he had never walked all the way to that eastern edge, to the source. That seemed significant, but it could also mean nothing.

Systems of thought, the chains of the mind. Easy to get lost. He needed to focus on his shoveling.

Good scrape of dirt. That was what he could rely on. In the moonlight, he could watch now as the dirt fanned out to either side of the shovel. He could shape the edges. Patterns that might be read.

The work was a good thing, good to have a distraction. He finished this wall and moved to the eastern wall where the furrow had never been finished, where he'd hit the untilled earth and stopped.

She had never tried to dig her way out. Pointless furrow, and pointless now to remove it. Who would care if some dirt were piled along part of a shed wall? But what he was really trying to do, he knew, was pass time. And so he slotted the shovel in along the wall, moved his good hand lower on the handle, then pulled slowly and walked backward, spread the earth. Looked at the edges like a wake in water, ran the shovel lightly along each side to smooth. He didn't want to see her, didn't want to find her. He wanted to put that off as long as possible.

But the furrow ended. Before long, there was no furrow left to remove, and it was still night, the moon higher now, small and distant and sliding away. Well, Galen said. There was no more work to do on the shed, except removing the lock, and that would have to come later. So he went to the pile on the lawn.

He had meant to burn this, but that would draw too much attention. He would bring the drawers out here, one at a time, fill them with crap, and slide them back in place. No one would ever know the difference.

So he did that. Labor. Walk out with a drawer, kneel on the grass, scoop piles of clips and rubber bands and old knobs and buttons, the family, pieces of family and time, and let them fall into the drawer. Reordered now, confused and moved, items returned to different locations, a disruption of pattern, but had there ever been any pattern? Disruption or fate. It was never clear. We did what we did, and wondered, and that was it. Blind movements in a void.

The crumpled photos would not fit into the drawers. And they wouldn't go back into the albums, obviously. So he wasn't sure what to do. He knelt in the grass and looked at them in moonlight. They were his now, no longer hers, and so he needed to preserve. He tried to flatten them, but once photo paper was bent, it was bent, the creases white. Schatze a darker shape, a kind of bullet among the photos, an intruder, gone before Galen was born.

He gathered the photos, black-and-white blooms, and cradled them in his arms, walked upstairs to his room and let them fall into his closet. Then he closed the door and they were gone. As simple as that.

What was left was her room. Clothing everywhere on the floor. Hangers loose, and he rehung her dresses, coats, shirts. Arranged them neatly in order, from longest to shortest. Felt the fabrics, smooth and cool to the touch. The colors bright. Turquoise and pink. This room would become a kind of museum, and he would visit to remember her, so it was important to put everything away carefully now.

A life could be contained in such a small space. Forty-six years in one room. Sacred room. When the floor was clean and everything hung, Galen bundled her blanket and sheets into a ball, walked out to the lawn and shook them in moonlight to remove the dirt, felt like a criminal. While everyone else slept, he was out here whipping sheets in the air, removing all sign of what had happened. Not as if he'd had a choice, though. The thing about a path was that it always led somewhere, and we could never pause on any path. We were always moving.

Galen carried the sheets and blanket to the pantry, to the washing machine. Watched the water fill, poured in detergent, and closed the lid.

It was the middle of the night, but Galen decided to fix lemonade, with real lemons, the way his mother had. He walked out to the small lemon trees along the hedge. The giant fig tree dwarfing all else, casting shadows as the moon went down, large leaves like paw prints against the side of the shed, some mythic beast passing without sound.

Galen felt hunted, exposed, unsafe. He grabbed an armful of lemons and hurried back into the house, focused on his task and tried to think of nothing else. Cut the lemons in half and ground them down against the juicer, poured each time it was full. Added water, added sugar, stirred with the long glass handle and bulb.

He poured himself a glass and sat at the table. On display for anything that might look in from outside, and he would not hear the approach because of the sound of the washer. He tried to enjoy the lemonade, but soon enough he was flicking off the light. He couldn't return to the table. He held his glass and stepped back into a dark corner from which he could look out. Nothing could come from behind.

The chugging of the washer obscenely loud. A suck and slosh. Galen stood in the darkness and watched and waited.

The house impossibly large. Nowhere to hide within it. Too many windows and doors. A hundred things could be waiting in here and he'd never know. Too risky, even, to try to get to the stairs. Galen wanted daylight. Darkness connected all places at once and magnified the vacuum in his ears and the thumping of his heart.

The house did not feel inanimate. It had played a role in all that had happened here. And Galen wished he could see ahead. If he brought his grandmother home, that might appease the house. Wood could return to wood.

Galen set his glass quietly on the floor and moved slowly along the wall toward the stairs. The washer a thing insane, bucking and chugging, calling too much attention to this place, drawing everything from any quieter place outside.

Galen ran. He ran around the corner and up the stairs into his mother's room, closed the door and locked it, then panicked that something was in here with him. He batted at the wall for the light switch but didn't find it, felt something behind him and could hardly breathe, then hit the switch and turned and crouched and saw nothing.

The room bright, her bare mattress, uncovered bed, and everything placed neatly in her closet and on the shelves. Her room the way it had always been, and he didn't know how he could have been so jumpy. Fear of the dark was the opposite of transcendence. The exact opposite. The worst direction possible. Cavemen cowering near the fire, looking over a shoulder, listening for the snap of wood. Fear of the dark was full belief in the world, full enslavement, and it meant there had been no progression. Somehow, all that he had learned was not accumulating. Instead of approaching a goal, he was appearing in flashes and then vanishing again, with no control over where he might appear next.

Galen slowed his breath and walked over to his mother's bed and lay down. He would keep the light on, he knew. That helpless against himself, that ruled by nothing.

n the morning, Galen stood at the lock. He inserted a crowbar and could see that he'd be tearing down the entire shed and digging a hole in the earth before that lock would break. And a lock was not a bad thing, really, to keep people out.

The morning the same as any other, exactly the same, the air heating, shadows knitting themselves up toward noon. The last day of his ordeal, but the external world was indifferent. He was going to finish before night came again, even if the world didn't care.

Galen walked around to the toolshed. This might be his way in. If he cut through this interior wall, he could still lock the toolshed and there'd be no outward sign.

So he cleared away the last of the tools, grabbed an axe, and swung at the wood, swung high on the wall at an angle to cut across a board, and the blade sank deep and stuck. He tugged at the handle, and he could get it to seesaw back and forth a bit, but it wasn't coming out, and it was too high on the wall for him to pull directly. Damn it, he said.

He looked around for another axe. All these tools flung across the dirt, and no second axe. The cabin had an assortment, but only one here.

Then he saw the pick. A miner's pick, something left over from the gold rush.

Galen stood before the wall in a wide stance, his right hand far down the handle to support that heavy end, and he swung with all his might into the wall. Aah, he yelled, and the narrow sharpened point of the pick went right through the wall, buried instantly to the shank, and he rapped his knuckles of both hands against wood.

Galen howled in pain, his left hand on fire. He staggered around in the furrows flapping the hand in its gauze and sucking at his breath, another dance in the orchard, a puppet on strings. He had no skills in this world.

The trees had no comment. Dulling in the sun, shrinking and hardening.

He danced until the searing faded enough that he could regain his mind and breath and walk back to the shed, to that wall. Two long handles hanging now, the axe at an angle and the pick straight down.

Nice, he said. The other end of the pick, sticking out, was a blade about three inches wide. So he had used the wrong end.

He looked around at the other tools, shovels and rakes. A few saws of different sizes and types, short thick handsaws for pruning, larger blades for cutting firewood, all useless because the gaps between boards were not wide enough to insert a saw crossways.

But there was a sledgehammer. A big fist of metal at the end of a stick, and that seemed right. That was perfect for how he felt. He'd tear down this patch of wall and then maybe just keep going.

His left hand did not want to grip a handle, but he made it grip, and he swung that metal high and hard as any lunatic Viking and heard wood crunch and the axe came loose, the blade twisting toward him, and he jumped to the side and watched it fall. Then he swung the sledgehammer again and broke through one of the boards, ancient shed buckling now, and the hammer caught and he had to step close to lift and pull it free.

Galen was breathing hard. Heavy hammer, and the air heating. Shattered plank, and he swung now at its neighbor, felt the lob of iron through space, felt the unstoppable force as it crunched through wood. Momentum. A hammer was a sign. It was fate and doom. It was exactly like the momentum of our lives. Impossible to stop a hammer once it was flung. All you could do was hold on and feel the impact.

The top of two boards broken, and he swung low now, to bash them at their roots. A croquet mallet. On the back lawn, in his childhood, they'd played on Sunday afternoons, bright red and blue balls and stakes, and his grandparents sitting at the white iron table beneath the fig tree. Something he hadn't remembered in so long. His mother in a sun hat that tied under her chin. Strange hat, from another time, as if his childhood had happened fifty years back or even a hundred years.

But memory was only distraction. He needed to wipe his mind free of memory, needed to focus on the swing of metal through air and into wood. Crunch of wood, and the plank vibrated, connected only at its middle, where it was nailed into a crossbeam. Galen moved on to its mate, smashed and smashed again until the two of them hung there quivering, the pick still hanging.

The problem with memory was that it told us whatever we wanted to hear. It had no shape of its own.

Galen dropped the sledgehammer, heavy thud and a rising of dust in the still air. He didn't know why there was no wind this summer. There had been wind other summers, but this one they were meant to rebreathe their own air, a gradual loss of oxygen and thought. Nothing to do this summer but lose your mind.

I need a saw, Galen said. He could saw the crossbeam through the narrow gaps between planks and cut these two planks free. But he missed the sledgehammer already, liked the feel of its power, so he picked it up again, even though there was no chance of breaking through the beam behind the planks.

Galen swung hard and the impact blasted his hands, too solid and unforgiving. He dropped the sledgehammer and had to breathe fast until the sharp pain in his mangled hand became only a throb again. Dust in his nostrils.

He stepped out of the toolshed and looked at all the tools spread across the ground. As if the earth were offering the tools directly, grown from soil. The tools the color of soil, worn brown wood and faded iron.

He selected a pruning saw with jagged teeth. Short thick handle like an antique pistol, Galen a conquistador, stepping back almost five hundred years. He was supposed to use a regular handsaw, he knew, the kind for cutting firewood, but he liked the look and feel of this one. It would catch and snag, and that seemed right. He wanted it to be difficult to get into the shed.

He slid the blade between planks and brought it down against the beam, pulled back to cut the first groove. Pushed forward and the blade stuck, wouldn't move at all. So he lifted and set it in place again and pulled back to form a deeper groove, the sawdust a light yellow, and pushed forward again and stuck. Yet another sign. Like gravity, like the failure of progression. Pulling back always easy, moving forward always blocked.

Galen's energy for battle was waning. He dropped the pruning saw and went outside for a regular handsaw with a wide blade and small teeth, the saw he should have begun with originally. And this one worked much more easily. Push and pull, light at first, then digging in, sawdust so fine he was breathing it.

He was through that beam in no time, and it collapsed onto the

saw blade, some force of the shed falling inward, so he had to yank
the saw free.

On to the next gap, the other side of his two hanging planks, and
he moved quickly, ripping the wood, and suddenly was through and
the two planks fell away from him into the shed, banged against the
tractor.

He realized now what he had done. The wall was down. The
shed no longer a cage.

Mom?

Darker in the shed, most of it in shadow, and his eyes in a panic,
looking everywhere, but nothing moved. He wanted there to be
movement. He wanted his mother to be alive.

The green tractor, the stacks of walnut racks, the dirt floor. But
no movement, and no sound except his own blood in his ears. Mom?

He wanted her to be alive. He hadn't expected that. He hadn't
expected that at all. He was afraid to step through the gap.

Galen felt like he was standing at the edge of the world, that if
he took one step forward he would fall off. He was swaying in place,
dizzy with vertigo, and he wanted to step back, away from the edge,
and get down low on the ground.

But he stepped forward, into the shed, and the ground did not
fall away. It held his feet and he was in here with his mother now
and he didn't know where she was. Mom?

He was afraid to look around. His eyes would look down at the
floor, along a wall, searching for her, but then up at the ceiling, all
too fast to register anything. He didn't want to see.

The shed larger inside than he had remembered, and it seemed
to be growing, the walls receding.

He stepped around the front of the tractor, his left hand on its
snout for balance. He could be sucked away in a vacuum at any
moment.

Dread. A physical presence to it. He did not want the moment of finding her. Looking down and then looking away, shadows everywhere, each of them his mother for a moment and then nothing.

He stayed close to the tractor, didn't want to venture farther into the shed. The broken racks waiting behind the tractor, some of them waiting decades now, unmoved. He picked one up, dusty wood and an old metal screen, torn in the center, and carried it to the empty space in front of the tractor. Then he picked up another and carried it to the same place, began a new stack.

The route from old stack to new stack, held together by the tractor. Galen focused on the screens, the wood he had expected to be cool to the touch, but it was warm. The shed no real shelter at all. The air felt as hot as outside. He didn't know how that could be. A place of shade, but perhaps the roof and walls baked and became an oven, heating the trapped air.

Smell of walnut, old husks. Acidic and sharp, a green and black smell, and the smell of dust. The sound of heating, of the roof expanding.

Galen carried the screens, dozens of them, until the space behind the tractor was bare dirt, old dirt unexposed since his mother's childhood. Older dirt smelled more like rock. He would dig here.

He stepped outside through the toolshed for the shovel, emerged in the bright light, squinting. Found a shovel with a good tip and stepped back inside.

Galen set the shovel and pushed hard with his foot, and the shovel buried partway in. But when he pulled up, there was not much on the blade. This could take a very long time.

He went for the pick, pulled it free of its board leaning against the tractor. He swung at the earth with the larger blade end, and the impact was too hard, too much resistance, so he tried the other end, a long curved spike, the one that had punctured the board, and this dug deep and easily, without stunning his hands. He lifted up on the handle and walked forward to rip the spike through the earth, loosening the dirt.

Dirt was inescapable. Always a return to dirt. Galen stabbed again and again, breaking the surface in an oval six feet long and two feet wide. It didn't need to be deep. He'd be putting the wooden screens back over the top.

Broken earth, old work, heaving iron. Who he was no longer mattered. A question from an earlier time. Grave digger. Mother grave digger.

Each time the pick hit, the buried smell of the earth was released, the smell of decades past, of the earlier shed and his mother playing here as a girl. The work of his grandfather and whoever else had come before.

Galen shaped an oval as lovely as a stained-glass window. An oval of ruptures. And then he dropped the pick and raised the shovel. He buried the blade carefully, scooped the loose clods and grains and set them aside in a neat pile graveside.

Shovelful and shovelful. Sound of it. Drips of his sweat mixing in. All labor took longer than we thought. A small oval, small window, and yet it was more than it seemed, and the pile already becoming larger than he expected, even for this shallow first level, this bare beginning.

T he digging its own eternity, a place where time collapsed. The dirt knew what it was making room for.

Scraping with the shovel, gathering the last of what he had loosened, and then swinging the pick again, hearing the tap against rock, soil impregnated with rock. Soil not meant for planting.

Caving away beneath him. Deepest cave, digging the grave of one's own mother. This was why the world rushed away on all sides. Without the mother, the container of the world no longer held.

His thoughts in a panic, no still point anywhere. Rushing like the earth and the air. Wanting to look behind him, wanting to find her, needing to see whether she was still alive, but unable to move from this one point, struggling to stand on safe ground.

The pick large, the handle like bone, expanded, hollow inside, difficult to hold on to. Darker soil now, older soil. He was passing beyond the time of his family, crossing into an earlier time.

The meaning of dirt was this, perhaps. The shovel removing time. The eons it took to form the dirt from rock. The water and air that had to work through millions or even billions of years to free it, and then its travel and settling and waiting, layer upon layer. His life now such a brief flash. Any attachment was absurdity. This was what the dirt taught. If he could remain focused on geologic time, human time could never reach him.

The shovel willing, always willing. And the dirt itself. Waiting for so long, yet no resistance to being moved. All order upset, the arrangement of grains, but no resistance and therefore no suffering.

The pile along one side of the grave, spilling right to its edge. The dirt became larger once it was removed. A dark mountain range forming. Another layer scraped and cleared, and he wondered whether she could hear this sound. He didn't like not knowing whether she could hear. He kept glancing behind him, kept expecting to see her standing there, walking toward him.

He worked as quickly as he could. He did not want to continue into night.

The ground became harder still, rockier and bound together. A large stone shuddering through his hands when the pick hit, and he had to shovel around it, clear away a few inches on every side, gray face and white scar from the pick, then get down in the grave on his hands and knees and pull at it, clawing through the gloves, trying to get a grip, until he was able to hug it onto his lap. Heavy stone, and he could use it to mark her grave. He'd leave it at one end, with that mark from the pick, his mark, and no one else would know, but this would work as a headstone.

Galen shuffled on his knees with the rock held in his lap, scooted to the head of the grave, and rolled the stone up to ground level. Smooth stone, smooth face, old river stone somehow arrived here, so far from water.

Galen stood inside the grave, as deep as his knees now. He swung the pick from here. It doesn't need to be deep, he told himself, but he imagined it not deep enough and having to reach down to pull her from the grave, having to lift her in his arms.

So he kept swinging the pick, bit deep into another layer, and the day was an inferno but the ground was cooler down low, had its own breath. Cutting through layers, this labor like cutting through the illusion of self to find there was no core, only the layers.

Rockier, the pick shuddering and deflecting. Sparks. A miner.

He stepped to the other end, soft and chewed earth now, his feet sinking, and he swung at where he had stood before. He would step back and forth, two sides of a mirror, lowering slowly down.

The dirt almost moist. Darker and heavier and not quite damp but almost. He'd thrown off his shirt and was covered in dirt, restored. Lifting shovelful after shovelful, the pile so enormous he had to start using the other side.

And he could have gone on forever, perhaps, digging down and down, because that was better than facing what had to be done next, but eventually he had to admit to himself this was deep enough. Deeper than his waist, and he didn't need more than that. The afternoon moving on, and he was not willing to be here after dark.

So he rose out of the grave and took a few steps into the rest of the shed and then stopped. Unreliable ground. He took a few more steps to the edge of a row of racks, and he knew that if he walked from here to the eastern wall he would find her. That was where he'd found the checkbook, and that would be where she had lain down. He felt sure of that. His eyes fully adjusted after all this time digging, so he would not be saved by any shadows.

Three rows of racks he'd have to pass, and she could be anywhere.

Beyond the first row was nothing but ground. Everything accelerating away from him, a void without sign, his mind emptied.

And beyond the second row, he again saw nothing. He felt he would topple. The dread overwhelming now, a funneling down toward fate with only one row left and no choice to be made, ever.

He stepped past the final row of racks. His mother, lying on the ground, facedown in the dirt. Almost peaceful, her head resting on an arm that was outstretched, hand loose. She was wearing an apron over her skirt and blouse. He hadn't remembered that. The day she'd gone into the shed seemed so long ago, an eternity, a time when they both were different people, irrecoverable now. An apron with flower faces on the front, an apron from his earliest memories.

Galen was aware that he should feel something. He stood in place, his arms awkward, hanging at his sides. He could feel himself tilting. Impossible to believe it was his mother lying there. And he didn't know that she was dead. He just couldn't see any movement.

He needed to carry her to the grave. He needed to get out of here as quickly as possible. But all he could do was kneel down. He couldn't reach in close enough to pull her up. He didn't want her on his shoulder or against his chest.

Mom?

Galen hadn't made any plan for this moment. He had somehow managed to believe this moment was not coming.

He crawled closer to her and kept expecting her to move. He would call an ambulance if she moved. It was up to her. Mom?

She looked smaller than he remembered.

He was dizzy, even on his hands and knees, so he lay down, just for a moment, lay down on his side facing her. His breath was tight, but he tried to calm. It'll be okay, he said.

He closed his eyes. He was vaulting end over end through his chest, falling away to some distant point. A pull as each end flipped past the other. Where he was falling, he didn't want to go. Dark cavern, pressure walls, his own ribs compacting as they grew. Walls of blood and bone inflated, his body swelling, and he was falling through the center, shrinking.

But he couldn't afford to lie here. If someone came and found him now, the grave dug, lying beside his dead mother.

Galen opened his eyes and sat up. He shook his head. Move, he said. Get moving.

He grabbed her ankles, tried not to think of this body as his mother, just pulled and dragged, and her skirt rode up, her underwear exposed, and this was not what he wanted to see, so he dropped her legs, walked around to her head, grabbed her arms, pulled them free until he had her wrists, small wrists, her body more limp than it should have been, no rigor mortis, the flesh not cold, and he panicked. She might still be alive.

He dropped her arms, stood there breathing hard, looking for movement. But there was no movement. It was just hot in this shed. That's why she wasn't cold. And that's why she wasn't stiff. Just the heat of this shed.

He should check for breath, but he didn't want to kneel down and put his ear to her mouth. So he picked up her wrists again and dragged her limp body toward the pit. He dragged as fast as he could. She was heavy.

He dragged and looked behind him at the ground. He would not look at her. Passing the rows of racks.

His hands on her wrists, and he kept imagining a pulse, tried to focus instead on the ground. The weight of her, like his own body grown, an enormous distended belly dragging over the earth. A creature doomed to walk forever backward, legs weak and struggling, narrow spine straining, lungs too small. A thing that would never rest. Dragging half dead across this dirt and farther still, perhaps, into the furrows and orchard, dry grass, black rock, volcanic. Dragging this load on and on as the crust opened and filled itself and grew. Just like in my dreams, he said.

But he kept pulling, and when he came to the pit, he dragged her along the side with less dirt and she tilted along that loose dark mound and rolled and fell down in unintended and he had to let go. Damn it, he said.

Galen didn't know how he had intended to place her in the grave, but not like this, rolling out of control and bunched up in a heap at the bottom, facedown.

He needed to straighten her out and get her faceup, but he did not want to get down there in the grave with her.

The shovel was all he could think of. He stood in the loose dirt at the edge and leaned over and tried to pull at her legs with the shovel, but there was nothing to hook on to. The shovel slipping along her thighs.

He needed something that could grab. Something for reaching into trees to get walnuts or fruit, some picker. He walked out into the late-afternoon sun, bright still, and shielded his eyes, scanning the dirt for some long tool with a hook. He imagined a lever or a string or something, some grabber.

But such a tool did not exist. He was squinting and blinking and stumbling around in the dirt, and he did not have what he needed. Then he saw a hoe, a solid blade, and another hoe with four tines and space between. Like the pitchfork, but bent at ninety degrees. He could grab with that.

Back inside, his eyes were no longer adjusted. The grave was dark, his mother hidden in shadow. He knelt down in the pile of dirt and used the hoe or rake or whatever it was—a rake, maybe— and tried to catch one of her knees. If he could catch a knee, he could straighten out that leg.

He was in danger of falling in, though, off-balance, and that would be a nightmare, so he got up off his knees and straddled the grave, one foot on each side. That was better. He was at one end, the end for her feet, and was able to reach down with the rake and troll for her legs.

Galen caught a knee and carefully straightened, wondering again about rigor mortis and why that wasn't happening, and then he caught the edge of the other thigh and pulled up, but that leg was trapped. She was bunched up with her butt in the air and her arms under her, and the whole thing was just a mess.

His feet were buried in the loose piles of dirt, the grains settling in the tops of his sneakers, and he felt claustrophobic, everything closing in around him. He stepped down into the grave, knelt on either side of her legs, and the entire world was collapsing in toward him, grains coming down over the edges of the grave, and he needed to hurry before he was buried along with her.

He dug his hands under her body, working along the cool earth, leaned forward, embracing her, and pulled to turn her over as gently as he could.

Her legs and hips facing upward now, and he scooted higher, worked his arms fully around until he could ease her onto her back and was holding her close. He lay his face against her breast. He would rest here a moment. Mom, he said.

His breath tightened and shook and the sobbing rocked his chest. He had never wanted his mother to die. She was all he had.

Mom, he said, and the grief was more than he'd expected. He needed to remember that she wasn't real, that she was only an illusion, manifested here to teach him. His final attachment. There was no longer anything to hold him to this world, and that was right. That was good and necessary.

She was still warm, her breast still warm. I love you, he said. Thank you for coming in to my life. I honor you. Mother. He let there be a ceremonial pause and then said it again. Mother.

He held her as tightly as he could in his arms, and he imagined he could hear a heartbeat, but he knew it was only his own blood and breath.

Mom, he said, and he let himself cry, let himself sob and weep, didn't try to hold back anymore, pressed close against her, and now he thought he really did hear a heartbeat, and he sat up quickly.

He sat still and listened, as if he might hear it again through the air, and then he stood and got out of that grave quick and grabbed the shovel and tossed a load of dirt onto her, but a shovelful was not enough. This was not fast enough.

Galen lunged at the biggest pile on his hands and knees. A mountain range that he needed to move. He braced his feet against a tractor wheel to push with his chest and both arms, turning himself into a plow, filling the grave. Her face and upper body gone now, the dirt already deep, and he shifted to the side, braced against the other wheel, collapsed the next mountain. He was a giant, forming the earth, deciding what the world would be. Origins. Coming closer to origins, another gift of the dirt. A cataclysm of earth, centuries high, spilling down over her stomach and hips and legs and feet, and even after she was gone, he kept pushing, inhaled the good breath of dirt, felt it caked in his eyes and mouth, taste of time, of the accumulation of time and its release, and felt his hands like claws.

ACKNOWLEDGMENTS

'd like to thank the John Simon Guggenheim Memorial Foundation and the University of San Francisco for generous support during the writing of this novel, and Colm Tóibín, Janet Burroway, and David Kirby for recommending me.

I'd also like to thank Jason Arthur at William Heinemann, Peter Straus, Catherine Eccles, and everyone at Inkwell, especially Kim Witherspoon, David Forrer, Lyndsey Blessing, and Alexis Hurley.

And I must of course thank Galen Palmer, my best friend in high school, whose name I've borrowed here. Early on, he was the one who helped turn my life around.